Reverend Mother Ann put down her cup and smiled again. Oddly enough, it was when she smiled, revealing small and undoubtedly natural teeth, that one became aware that she was no longer a very young woman. The smile revealed tiny lines round nose and mouth, a faint darkening of the flesh beneath the fine, slanting eyes.

"Now I must interview our new novice," she said, rising. "You travelled with her on the train. How did she strike you?"

"As a very nice, eager, sincere girl," Sister Joan said promptly.

"Untouched?"

"I beg your pardon, Reverend Mother?"

"Would you judge her to be a virgin still?"

"Well, one cannot tell merely from looking," Sister Joan said in bewilderment.

A VOW
OF
SILENCE

Veronica Black

IVY BOOKS • NEW YORK

Ivy Books
Published by Ballantine Books
Copyright © 1990 by Veronica Black

All rights reserved under International and Pan-American Copyright Conventions. Published in the United States by Ballantine Books, a division of Random House, Inc., New York. Originally published in Great Britain by Robert Hale Limited in 1990.

Library of Congress Catalog Card Number: 89-77808

ISBN 0-8041-0814-5

This edition published by arrangement with St. Martin's Press, Inc.

Manufactured in the United States of America

First Ballantine Books Edition: January 1992

ONE

✠ ✠ ✠

Sister Joan's least favourite hour of the day was the hour of recreation sandwiched between supper and Benediction. In one sense it justified its name since all that the members of the Community did was to recreate the events of the day in minute and tedious detail from Sister St. Jude having lost and found her spectacles to Sister Patrick having seen a cloud in the shape of an angel. As Sister St. Jude lost her spectacles somewhere or other every day and as Sister Patrick was always seeing angels—often in places where no self-respecting angel would have touched down—conversation lacked sparkle. Reverend Mother Agnes seldom attended the recreation on the grounds that the novices would find it more difficult to relax with the eagle eye of the Prioress on them. Sister Joan suspected, however, that Reverend Mother Agnes found the period as tedious as she did herself.

Now she smiled modestly for the ten thousandth time as Sister Clare said, "Such beautiful embroidery, Sister Joan! If it were not a sin I might be quite envious of your talents."

"We all have certain talents to be used for the glory of God," Sister Francis said. Sister Francis could be

1

relied upon to state the obvious. The faint reproach in her voice was there to remind them that personal compliments were not encouraged.

"It would be a great help if the Lord let me know what my particular talent is," Sister Edith said wistfully. Sister Edith was large, well meaning and clumsy. Her cooking was abominable; her cleaning enthusiastic but slapdash; her voice tuneless. She approached every task assigned to her with grim determination but so far her particular metier had eluded detection. Sister Joan considered the suggestion that Sister Edith might have the virtue of forcing her companions to practise charity and patience, but the remark would have been unkind. In any case the moment had passed. Sister Patrick was drawing their attention to a faint stain on the wall that looked like the outline of a cherub. Several of the others professed to see the resemblance too which was hardly surprising since a wall relief depicting a cherub had been removed for cleaning not long before, an event which they all seemed to have failed to notice.

A discreet tap on the door announced Sister Clement, one of the two lay sisters. The two lay sisters didn't often attend the recreation hour either since they were required to man the outside telephone, run any last-minute errands needed before Benediction, and type out the duty roster for the next day.

"Dominus vobiscum," Sister Clement said.

"Et cum spiritu tuo. What is it, Sister Clement?" Sister Francis who was in charge of the recreation looked an enquiry.

"Reverend Mother's compliments and will Sister Joan please go and see her?"

A summons to see Reverend Mother Agnes during recreation was not unusual. The Prioress often took advantage of the period to have a quiet talk with one or another of her Community, to give news from home, or discuss doubts and difficulties concerning vocations, or occasionally to reprimand in decent privacy some fault that might shock the novices if it were commented on in general confession.

Sister Joan was already folding up her cushion cover though she paid Sister Francis the courtesy of a murmured,

"By your leave, Sister?"

"Certainly, Sister Joan." Sister Francis inclined her head graciously.

A summons from the Prioress was expected to be obeyed promptly. Once outside the recreation room Sister Joan glided briskly in the direction of the parlour.

Parlour was actually a misnomer since the main parlour where visitors were admitted was situated at the other side of the building. The smaller room where the Prioress spent much of her time was never glimpsed by the general public who would not have recognised the bare and austere apartment as being a parlour at all.

Reverend Mother Agnes matched the austerity of her surroundings, her long face and aristocratic hands giving her a strong resemblance to an El Greco stepped out of his frame, with only her sweet, clear voice to impart femininity to her aspect. Her habit, of dark purple to denote her position in the Community, was cut on economical lines; beneath the white wimple her long, pale eyes surveyed the younger woman without emotion as Sister Joan entered with the customary,

"Dominus tecum."

"Et cum spiritu tuo. Close the door and sit down, Sister Joan."

As usual the younger woman was intrigued by the contrast between the harsh masculinity of her appearance and the bell-like clarity of her voice. Someone had whispered to her once that Reverend Mother Agnes had given up a promising career to enter the religious life.

She would not have been surprised to learn that it was true, but she was unlikely to learn it from the Prioress herself who kept the rule of silence about one's previous existence conscientiously.

"I apologise for interrupting your recreation, Sister," Reverend Mother Agnes said now, resting her folded hands on the flat-topped desk at which she was sitting.

"It was not wildly exciting, Reverend Mother," Sister Joan said dryly.

Usually her remarks caused the long, thin mouth of her superior to twitch, but tonight Reverend Mother Agnes remained grave.

"You have been with us for five years," she said.

"From when I entered the religious life," Sister Joan said.

The Prioress had just begun on her second term of office, it being the rule in the Order of the Daughters of Compassion that no sister might serve more than two consecutive five-year terms as Prioress.

"There is a vacancy in our House in Cornwall," Reverend Mother Agnes said.

Another rule of the Order stipulated that no more than fifteen professed nuns and lay sisters should comprise one House. In an age of dwindling vocations this necessitated some juggling of inmates.

"I am sorry if it is bad news," Sister Joan said.

"Good news though not as the world sees it. Mother Frances passed away peacefully in her ninety-first year. She was my own Novice Mistress many years ago. A very fine woman. May her soul—"

"And the souls of all the faithful departed through the mercy of God rest in peace," Sister Joan chimed in, crossing herself.

"Reverend Mother Ann has written to enquire if we can spare them a sister," Reverend Mother continued.

"And you want me to go?"

The voice was convent calm but Sister Joan's dark blue eyes had flashed mutinously. After five years she still had not complete command of her eyes.

"For the last three months ever since Sister Jane made her full profession we have been one in excess of the rules," Reverend Mother said without reproach. "Who goes is, of course, my responsibility. I have thought deeply about it. I have decided that you are the one most fitted. I wish to send someone I can trust absolutely, someone who is not tied hand and foot by convention."

Sister Joan sat up straighter, the spark of rebellion becoming a spark of interest.

"I don't quite follow you, Reverend Mother," she said cautiously.

"You don't follow me because I am not yet leading you anywhere," the other said. "Last month I received a letter from Mother Frances. We did exchange letters once or twice a year. She was in the habit of keeping in touch with all her former novices. She saw it as her duty. The letter troubled me very much. I did not answer it since I was unsure how to answer it."

That Reverend Mother Agnes should confess herself uncertain was unique in Sister Joan's experience.

"Perhaps you had better read it for yourself," she was saying, sliding a piece of paper across the desk.

The handwriting was the delicate italic script of a nun who has grown old in the cloister, with a faint shakiness here and there.

"In the Name of Our Blessed Lord,
  "My dear Mother Silence,
    "You will forgive your old Novice Mistress for addressing you by your old nickname, I claim the privilege of age. My felicitations on your nearing

the end of your second term of office. I too am
nearing the end and trust soon to be elected into a
higher sphere. I count myself blessed that my intellect remains clear though my old enemy, migraine, troubles me occasionally. I think often of
the pleasant recreations we used to have under
Mother Celeste. It is a sign of age, is it not, when
the past becomes clearer than the present? I know
you will excuse the evil writing. How I wish I had
the penmanship of dear Sister Bridgit O'Reilly. You
remember her, I trust?

"If circumstances enable you to visit I shall look
forward eagerly to what we both must realise will
be the last time.

"Yours Affectionately in Our Lord,
"Mother Frances Byrne."

Having read it through twice Sister Joan looked up,
her small face puzzled. "Forgive me, Reverend Mother,
but I don't see—" she began.

"Mother Frances had a rooted horror of nick-
names," the Prioress said. "She certainly never bestowed any upon her novices. I believe the salutation
enjoins discretion upon me."

"About what?"

"She gives no hint of that." Reverend Mother Agnes
took back the letter and tapped it with a long forefinger.
"What she speaks about in this makes no sense at all. She
never suffered from migraine headaches in her life. During my novitiate I was the one troubled by migraine. And
the recreation periods under Mother Celeste were the opposite of pleasant. Mother Celeste, God rest her soul, was
of the opinion that the Inquisition ought never to have been
abolished."

Sister Joan choked back a giggle. This was not, she
sensed, a time for levity.

"Finally she calls to mind the penmanship of Sister Bridgit O'Reilly. Sister Bridgit was a lay sister during my novitiate. A very good, sincere girl, completely illiterate."

The blue eyes fixed on her opened more widely.

"Is it possible," Sister Joan said after a moment or two, "that Mother Frances was going senile?"

"Senility does not write a short, coherent letter, in which as much misinformation as possible is crowded into as brief a space as possible," the Prioress said. "I believe that Mother Frances was trying to convey to me that all was not well. I also suspect that whatever was troubling her could not be confided to Reverend Mother Ann."

Reverend Mother Ann would have read the letter in accordance with regulations.

"You say that you didn't answer this, Reverend Mother?"

"I delayed." There was regret in the pretty voice. "I read it over several times, trying to work out the best plan of action. Finally I telephoned the convent and enquired after Mother Frances. I was informed her long life was moving peacefully to its close, and that had I travelled to see her it is very doubtful if she would have rallied sufficiently to recognise me. A few days ago I received word of her death. It was announced, Sister." Sister Joan blushed slightly. Announcements of professions, of anniversaries and of deaths in the various Houses of the Order were read out during supper, and for her own part she often permitted her mind to wander.

"I feel that I ought to have responded to the letter, perhaps set her mind at rest," the Prioress said. "I dislike unfinished business, Sister."

"You want me to become part of the Cornwall Community?"

"Reverend Mother Ann has requested one of my professed sisters. She wants one who can undertake teaching duties. You have a Diploma, do you not?"

"Only in Art and Literature, Reverend Mother."

"I presume you can make shift to teach other subjects?"

"Yes, Reverend Mother."

Again the meek answer, the flash of the blue eyes.

"You are thirty-five years old, are you not? Yours was a late vocation."

"Between the saddle and the ground," Sister Joan said with a sudden, disarming grin.

"You lived enough in the world to acquire a certain sophistication, an impatience with the conventional way of doing things. You are also alert and efficient." The blue eyes were raised to the long face opposite.

"I have no relish for intrigue," the younger woman said bluntly.

"Meaning that when you enter the Cornwall House your first loyalty must be to your new sisters? Your first loyalty must be to God, child, and if there is some wrong, some injustice He wishes to be discovered then it is your duty to discover it."

"And report it to you?"

"When you leave here my authority over you ceases," the Prioress said, "so I must leave it to your own good judgement to decide what is to be done should there be anything—shall we say irregular?"

"May I ask what Reverend Mother Ann is like?" Sister Joan said.

"I have never personally met her," the Prioress said disappointingly. "I know her only by reputation. She is reputed to have a brilliant mind. Her father was Professor Gillespie, the noted archaeologist. I understand that as a girl she accompanied him on several of his digs. When he died she entered the religious life. I also understand that the Benedictines were very disappointed that she didn't choose them. Our own Order is comparatively modest. We do not even have the distinction of having been founded by a saint, though it is my hope that in her own good time Rome will remedy that.''

She glanced as she spoke towards a framed photograph on the wall. The thin, bright-eyed gaze of the young woman who gazed out from the frame held the attention of the most casual observer. It could have been the face of a mystic or of a fanatic, the eyes blazing into some private vision, the lower lip drooping and vulnerable.

"They say she had many lovers," the Prioress said. "There was considerable opposition when she founded her first convent, many asking quite reasonably why she was not content to join one of the existing Orders, but she wanted to leave her individual stamp upon the religious life. Well, she got her way. If she wishes to be raised to the altars she will get her way in that too. As she stood in line for the gas chamber she called out that they would remember her. Twenty-eight years old with a life crammed full of incident behind her. Sister Joan, am I to send you to Cornwall?''

She was bending the rule, giving the other a choice.

"When would you wish me to leave?" Sister Joan asked.

"I can telephone them tomorrow and tell them to expect you on Saturday. You will want to write to your family and inform them of your change of address.''

"Yes, Reverend Mother." Sister Joan rose and gave the customary bow.

"You will be travelling down with a new novice," the Prioress informed her. "A very nice child of nineteen has decided to enter our Order. As we have our quota of eager hopefuls she will enter the Cornwall

House. One of their novices left recently so there is a space.''

A space into which the girl of nineteen might or might not fit. At nineteen, Sister Joan thought, she had been in her first year at Art College, drunk on the new sights, colours, and personalities. Meeting Jacob.

It struck her now as a strange and ironic fact that they had met on the steps of the tiny chapel, she about to enter, he leaving with a portfolio of rapid, scintillating sketches underneath his arm. It had been a foretaste of their relationship.

''If there is anything to be discovered, Reverend Mother,'' she said, banishing memories of Jacob and his portfolio, ''how do I contact you? That is assuming that what I find cannot be communicated for some reason to Reverend Mother Ann?''

''The school where you will be teaching is not within the enclosure,'' the Prioress told her. ''It is a small private school for the children of those who live on Bodmin Moor. So you will have more freedom of movement than is usual. You will not, of course, take advantage of it unless it is absolutely necessary.''

A bell for Benediction began to ring. Sister Joan bowed again and went out, closing the heavy door softly, automatically smoothing down the skirt of her ankle-length grey habit.

The rest of the Community were filing into the chapel. The four novices (no House was supposed to accept more than four at one time) trotted past under the watchful eye of Mother Euphemia. All those who had served a term as Prioress were entitled to retain the prefix of ''Mother'' and to sew a narrow purple ribbon to the sleeve of their habit, one ribbon for each five-year term served. These apparently childish distinctions of dress were all a part of the minute detail that went to make up the religious life, like the blue habits and white bonnets of the novices.

"You must understand that you are preparing to leave the world," Mother Euphemia had told her on her own arrival five years before. "The dress of the novices sets them apart from the professed and from the laity. During your novitiate you will begin to learn how it feels to be different from the majority."

The blue habit reached to mid-calf, showing thick black stockings and rubber-soled black shoes. Under the white poke bonnet her head had been shaven. She had never felt more ridiculous, nor realised more clearly her vanity.

The two years in the novitiate had been struggled through, to be followed by the vowing herself to poverty, chastity, obedience and compassion for one year. During that year her hair had been permitted to grow an inch, her poke bonnet exchanged for a white veil. At the end of the third year, despite a letter from Jacob, she had exchanged the blue habit for a grey one and taken perpetual vows.

In five years she had not left the convent. In five years she had not entered a shop, ridden on public transport, spoken with any man save the priest in the confessional. In five years she had not watched television, or read a newspaper, or listened to the radio.

"The two years after final profession must be years of solitude," the Prioress had said.

"You have been planted in a rich, but alien soil. Now you must take root there. Your talents are artistic and in this Order talents are to be employed and polished and perfected. What you must always do is to use those talents to the glory of God, always remembering that the religious life takes precedence. This is both an active and a contemplative Order. Only when you are secure in contemplation will you be able to take your full part in the active side of your vocation.''

The testing time was obviously considered to be over. In a couple of days she would be travelling down to Cornwall to join the Community there. Under Reverend Mother Ann Gillespie. The daughter of a brilliant archaeologist. Sister Joan tried to recall what she had read about him. He had made his name in the transcribing of Hittite inscriptions, had worked fairly intensively in the Near East, had been one of the experts called in to decipher the Dead Sea Scrolls, and had died shortly before his seventieth birthday. Whereupon his daughter had entered the Order of the Daughters of Compassion, a late vocation like her own, though probably not for the same reasons.

The star-shaped Monstrance containing the Holy Wafer was being lifted over the bowed heads of the congregation.

Sister Joan hastily bowed her own head, concentrating fervently on the blessing. After Benediction the bell clanged twice, heralding the grand silence that would last, barring emergencies, until six the following morning. In the world it was ten o'clock. Whatever old Mother Frances had been anxious about must concern the Prioress of the Cornwall House, otherwise she would have discussed the matter with her instead of writing a letter full of nonsense to her former novice. That was not to leap to the conclusion that what bothered her had any validity. Quite rational-seeming old ladies sometimes imagined they were being poisoned or imprisoned. Such old dears usually came out and complained about it openly though.

The Prioress stood at the door, asperging each exiting sister with a phial of holy water. Against the bare wall her shadow was thin and elongated, the padding of rubber-soled shoes the only sound.

Sister Joan knelt, felt the cool drops of water on her closed eyelids, opened her eyes to meet the cool, hooded gaze of her Superior.

Reverend Mother Agnes raised an eyebrow, looked an enquiry as clearly as if she had spoken it aloud.

"Am I prepared to go to the Cornwall House, to risk a division of loyalties should I find out something inimical to the Prioress there? After these two years of solitary work, of silence save during the hour of recreation, of no external stimuli, am I sufficiently in touch with my own capabilities to do this?"

She nodded her head almost imperceptibly, saw the wide thin mouth soften slightly, rose and filed out with the others.

TWO

✠ ✠ ✠

Sister Mary Salome had made the announcement, it being her turn this week to read out the notices during supper.

"Sister Joan has been appointed to our Cornwall House where Mother Frances recently passed over. Sister Joan will be teaching in the local school in addition to her religious duties. She will carry our good wishes and our prayers with her."

There was a murmur of approbation. Rather touching, Sister Joan thought, considering that they knew only the surface of her. Of the three novices who had entered with her two had left and the other gone to the mother House in Holland. What struggles of will and conscience she had endured were known only to Mother Euphemia and the Prioress. She doubted if her own experiences had been very different from all the other novices who had passed through their hands.

One or two curious, covertly envious glances were cast in her direction. Some of the women listening to the announcement would remain here for the rest of their lives. Not for them the journey by train down to the south-west tip of England.

"And I," Sister Joan thought, "will probably never come back here or see any of these people again."

The rule against making particular friendships was a sound one, breached at one's peril. Yet she felt a twinge of regret when she knelt for the blessing of the Prioress. Reverend Mother Agnes was a woman of character. There had been a subtle flattery in her request for help. She had not referred to the matter again. It was not in her nature to labour a point.

A taxi took her to the station. Had there been a local bus she would have been expected to take that in accordance with her vow of poverty. As it was she enjoyed the ride less than she had determined to do, because the well sprung plush interior startled a frame accustomed to stone floors and wooden benches, and the streets spun past too brightly coloured, too crowded with people. She supposed that someone emerging from prison might suffer from the same disorientation.

"Need any help, Sister?" The taxi-driver spoke in a self-consciously hearty way as if he were addressing a mental defective. Later he would go home and tell his wife that he'd taken one of the nuns to the station, and she'd seemed just like anybody else really.

"Thank you, no. I am meeting somebody."

He had already been paid and tipped. In her purse was her own ticket and five pounds in cash. She smiled at the taxi-driver, picked up her large suitcase in which her entire wardrobe was packed and went through on to the platform.

"Sister Joan?"

The voice was young and breathless, the face distractingly lovely.

"Veronica Stirling?"

It had to be. Sister Joan's blue eyes travelled swiftly over the blue coat and small hat pulled down over pale flaxen hair. The child had left off her make-up and elected to wear the most unbecoming garments she could find. She was still beautiful.

"I'm not late, am I, Sister? My parents wanted to come with me to see me off but I insisted on coming alone."

Parents could be a nuisance. Even the most fervently religious were apt to oppose the entry of a cherished daughter into the religious life. In her own case it had not been her parents but Jacob who had set stumbling blocks in her path.

"Very sensible of you, Veronica," she said briskly. "I see the train is in so we may as well find a couple of seats. Have you got your ticket?"

"Yes, Sister." Veronica produced it triumphantly.

"Come along then."

Having Veronica with her helped enormously through those first nervous moments when she showed her ticket, hauled her suitcase up to the rack and sat down. The compartment was empty. Sister Joan guessed that it might remain so, since most people avoided sitting next to nuns for journeys that lasted any length of time. Some Orders tried to circumvent this by updating the habit, shrinking the crucifix to the size of a lucky charm and trying to pretend there was no difference between nuns and laywomen. The Daughters of Compassion still wore the habits designed by their founder.

"We don't have to change, do we?" Veronica was asking, though she must have known the answer already. "I've never been to Cornwall, so it will be quite an adventure. Of course my family hoped that I could do my novitiate here, but I was told one of the novices in the Cornwall House left and there's a vacancy there. It probably is better to start out completely alone—so far as family is concerned, don't you think?"

"I think we ought to relax as we have a four-hour journey ahead," Sister Joan said, hoping she didn't sound stuffy. The child was nervous and overwrought and wanted to chatter, but she might as well begin learning that nobody made allowances for nerves in the religious life. Nobody made allowances for anything.

"Is it all right if I read?" Veronica said anxiously.

"As long as it isn't *I Leap Over The Wall*," Sister Joan said.

"Oh no, Sister." Veronica looked shocked. "It's St. Teresa's *Journal of a Soul*."

From the cover as she displayed it the journal was that of the Lisieux saint and not her Spanish namesake. The latter might prove strong meat for a wide-eyed romantic. She nodded approval, wondering if the girl would detect the sexual hysteria under the syrup, and decided that she probably wouldn't. Veronica seemed a young nineteen. Undoubtedly still a virgin which might be some kind of record.

The train screamed out. The other compartments had filled up, but the one in which they sat might as well have had a scarlet plague cross on the door. Sister Joan took out her Missal and, under cover of its closely written pages, let the miles slide past. April had drifted into a cool, wet May which boded ill for the summer ahead. She wondered what Bodmin would be like. There had been opportunities to go to Cornwall for artists' workshops when she was in college, but Jacob had vetoed them.

"Every fool who ever held a paintbrush rushes off to Cornwall. You and I are going to Sweden."

Cold, pearl-grey skies, white foam on green water, the light glinting on slippery fish-scaled cobblestones down at the quay, the sharp prow of a red fishing-boat. They had gone out together in one of the boats, huddling under a tarpaulin on deck while the rhythm of the work went on around them, instructions yelled in the sing-song of an unfamiliar tongue. She had never done better work than during that holiday nor felt more keenly the gap between talent and greatness.

"Would it be all right if I got a cup of coffee from the refreshments bar?"

She had forgotten that Veronica wouldn't be accustomed to long periods of fasting.

"Why not get two cups of coffee and some sandwiches?" she suggested, bringing out her purse.

"My treat," Veronica said brightly and whisked away.

The coffee was barely drinkable, the sandwiches surprisingly good. Wasting food was a sin. Sister Joan drank the coffee unflinchingly and longed for some thirst-crazed beggar to arrive and give her the chance to exercise charity. Thirst-crazed beggars were, however, in short supply on the Cornish line.

"Do you think I'll be allowed to telephone my parents to let them know that I've arrived safely?" Veronica asked, collecting the plastic and cardboard conscientiously.

"Someone will do that for you," Sister Joan said. "The initial break has to be a clean one, you know."

"Yes, of course."

In the end she had made the break herself, but not cleanly. She had left parts of herself like tattered rags in the wind in every place where she and Jacob had been. Five years and she was still not sure if the healing was complete.

Their compartment was no longer empty. A fat woman with a large shopping-basket got on the train and sat down two seats away from Sister Joan, her eyes roving over the other with ill-disguised curiosity. In a few minutes she would strike up a conversation, make some snide comment about women who locked themselves up to pray.

"You'll be going to the Daughters of Compassion, Sister." Her voice was rough but clear.

"Yes." Sister Joan hid her surprise.

"One or two of them used to visit the local hospital when I was having my veins done," the woman said. "Wonderful people. I'm not a Catholic myself but that made no difference. They always stopped by for a chat."

Sister Joan's hand rose, brushing the symbolic chip off her shoulder. It was something she had often teased Jacob about.

"He didn't short-change you just because you're Jewish. He probably cheats Moslems and Buddhists too."

They were coming at last into Bodmin. Slowing and stopping alongside a flower-bed edged with shells. The platform was slippery with rain.

"Reverend Mother Agnes said we would be met," Sister Joan said.

"There's a nun over there," Veronica said in the excited tones of a visitor to the South Seas who has just spotted her first grass skirt.

The sister flapped over to them, habit covered by a plastic cape and hood, wellingtons on the long feet.

"Our Lady be praised that you got here safely," a voice boomed from the depths of the plastic. "Perfectly foul weather. I'm Sister Felicity. Lay sister which gives me the chance to drive the car, though may I be forgiven for distinguishing it by that name. Give me your cases. Have you got your tickets? Right then, off we go."

All novices ought to be met by someone like Sister Felicity, Sister Joan thought, meekly following. In her presence introspection vanished. Anyone whose vocation consisted of romantic images of Audrey Hepburn looking impossibly beautiful would be speedily disillusioned by this cheerful normality.

The car was not a new model but neither was it the jalopy she had expected. It was sparklingly clean and the engine sounded well tuned. Sister Joan suspected that Sister Felicity spoke about it in the same way a proud mother often disparaged a clever child, to save both of them from the sin of pride.

"We're a fair way from the town," Sister Felicity was saying. "The House used to be the home of the local squire, you know. The family made their money in tin-mining. Then this century the family fortunes declined the way all fortunes decline, and the father of the present Tarquin—that's the family name—sold the place to the Order at a knockdown price. The son still lives here, built himself a more modern place. Still quite wealthy. Hold on."

The warning was unnecessary since she started up and accelerated smoothly away. She was obviously an excellent driver.

Sister Joan obeyed a gesture and snapped shut her seat-belt, glancing towards the back where Veronica sat with a faintly bemused expression on her face. Her more romantic notions were clearly being rapidly eroded.

"It's a real pleasure to have two newcomers," Sister Felicity said heartily. "One becomes insular. Did you ever meet Mother Frances?"

"No, never."

"Marvellous old soul," Sister Felicity said, negotiating a bend. "We have rather more than our share of old dears actually. Sisters Mary Concepta, Andrew and Gabrielle total nearly two hundred years between them. It will be a shot in the arm to get some fresh blood here."

"With us your House has its full quota, hasn't it?" Sister Joan asked.

"Fifteen professed, four novices," Sister Felicity nodded, spraying her passenger with raindrops from the brim of her plastic hood. Mid-forties, Sister Joan calculated, a gawky girl who had matured into a plain woman with intelligent eyes.

"That's the school where you'll be teaching." She waved a hand to the right.

Sister Joan had a glimpse of a low building set back from the narrow lane. Then they were past it, turning on to a broad track that made a wide, white parting on a low heath of short grass and tangled broom.

"It will mean a mile's walk twice a day," Sister Felicity said. "Do you like walking?"

"I used to love it."

"Because of the walking involved you're to be excused garden duty."

"Blessings never come singly," Sister Joan said piously.

"Here we are then." It was a shout of triumph as they sped off the track through open gates that led them on to a driveway bordered unexpectedly with sad-looking laurels.

The house looked exactly like the kind of Victorian monstrosity that a rich man without any aesthetic sensibilities might build. Basically it was well proportioned in the Elizabethan E shape, with two wings sweeping back from the ivied facade. It had probably been at a later date that someone had added the cupolas and columns and the huge greenhouse that was stuck on at one end of the front, ruining the symmetry.

"Marvellous old house, isn't it?" Sister Felicity said, drawing up before the double doors that marked the main entrance.

She wasn't trying to be funny. Her plain, strong face was glowing. She was as proud as if it were her own ancestral home.

Sister Joan was spared a reply since the doors were opened at that precise second and another lay sister, as short and plump as Sister Felicity was tall and thin, came down the half-dozen steps.

"Sister Joan? Veronica? Praise to Our Lady that you

got here. One hears such tales of the dangers of travelling on the railway these days. Come along. Sister Felicity will see to your bags. I'm Sister Margaret.''

They followed her into a cavernous hall in which a strip of red carpet looked uncannily like a tongue preparing to lick them up.

''Reverend Mother Ann will see you first, Sister Joan. Veronica, you are to come with me to meet Sister Hilaria, the Mistress of Novices.''

She indicated a small anteroom containing a carved wooden bench and bustled Veronica away.

Sister Joan stepped obediently into the antechamber and sat down on the bench, folding her hands.

The first meeting with one's Superior was important, setting the tone of future relationships. A good first impression could make a difference between having some private space in which to grow or being constantly frustrated by every pettifogging little rule and restriction a Prioress could dream up.

''Sister Joan, please come in.''

An inner door had swung silently open and the Prioress stood on the threshold, arms extended for the sexless embrace exchanged between sisters at arrival and departure.

''Reverend Mother Ann.''

First the bow and then the formal embrace. Two pairs of lips kissed the air at each side of the white veils.

The Prioress of the Cornwall House was tall and slim, her features regular. It was impossible to calculate her age from her smooth skin and dark eyes set slanting above high cheekbones. A classically beautiful woman, Sister Joan thought, with a definite charm of manner that might or might not be calculated.

''Come and sit down, Sister.'' The voice was warm, each word clearly enunciated. ''I always have a cup of herb tea at this hour, so I hope you will join me?''

The parlour must once have been the drawing-room when the Tarquin family had owned the house. The panelled walls had traces of gold paint still outlining the cornices. The floor of polished oak boasted two thin, exquisite Aubusson rugs, and the mullioned windows were diamond-paned. The few pieces of furniture obviously belonged to the house. Equally plainly they were valuable, two sofas covered with petit-point, two high-backed spool chairs, a multi-drawered cabinet against one wall inlaid with ivory, the table of walnut with a profusion of tiny plants carved about its edge. On one wall, between two of the windows, hung the photograph of the founder of the Order. In one corner between high Adam fireplaces and another window stood a carved wooden statue of the Holy Virgin, untinted, pristine in its simplicity.

"Shall we sit here?" The Prioress indicated two low basket chairs, of later date than the other furnishings, drawn up by a matching coffee-table on which two mugs of smoked glass were set. Steam curled up from them both and the spicy scent teased Sister Joan's nostrils.

She sat down, tensing slightly as she felt the plump cushion at her back.

"Did you have a comfortable journey, Sister Joan? It is a very long time since I was on a train. When my father was alive we travelled all over together, of course. Would you believe that I once learnt how to race a camel?"

Her dark eyes twinkled between their thick lashes.

"A horse is the most I ever rose to," Sister Joan confessed.

"But that is wonderful!" The other looked delighted. "We have a horse. Not a very challenging mount but a very affectionate, stable mare. She needs exercise, so you may ride her to and from the schoolhouse every day."

"But that would be wonderful." Sister Joan unconsciously echoed the other's phrase, then checked herself. "Is it allowed?"

"There is nothing in our rules which forbids a sister from riding a horse, though only lay sisters are permitted to drive cars. You can use a side-saddle? Good. I do not believe in interpreting the rules too rigidly."

She looked gently amused as she spoke. Sister Joan sipped her herb tea silently.

"Sister Felicia has probably told you that we have a number of elderly sisters here," the Prioress was continuing. "Three of them—Sisters Mary Concepta, Andrew and Gabrielle are in the infirmary most of the time. Of course their advice and wisdom are invaluable but they can no longer take an active role in the running of the convent. It puts more stress on the younger and more active among us. Fortunately we are a very happy little Community here. I will introduce you at suppertime. Now there must be questions you wish to ask me."

"Only about the school, Reverend Mother Anne. It's a Primary School for children who live on the moor. I didn't realise that people did live on the moor."

"Oh, there is the occasional isolated farm and the gypsies camp there regularly. The older children go by bus to the various Secondary Schools in the district, but many of the younger ones slip through the net. There is an excellent Primary School in Bodmin, but it is somewhat overcrowded. Mr. Tarquin senior endowed the moorland school in an attempt to provide some basic education for those who can't get into Bodmin, or whose schooling is frequently interrupted through family concerns. At sowing and harvest you will have very few pupils, I fear."

"It is not a State school then?"

"No, a private concern, but the teacher must be qualified, of course. You are?"

"I have a teaching diploma." She opened her bag and handed it over. "May I ask whom I am replacing?"

"Sister Sophia used to undertake the teaching. She died six months ago and her successor is unfortunately not fully qualified though she will continue to assist you as and when you deem necessary."

"Are we to take turns on the mare?" Sister Joan enquired.

The Prioress laughed.

"Sister David is terrified of any animal larger than a kitten," she said. "Were it left to her I'm afraid poor old Lilith would never get any exercise. No, when you require her at the school she will walk over as usual. She will be able to tell you much more about the routine and the pupils than I could. You will be able to ride over tomorrow after Mass to get your bearings."

She put down her cup and smiled again. Oddly enough it was when she smiled, revealing small and undoubtedly natural teeth, that one became aware that she was no longer a very young woman. The smile revealed tiny lines round nose and mouth, a faint darkening of the flesh beneath the fine, slanting eyes.

"Now I must interview our new novice," she said, rising. "You travelled with her on the train. How did she strike you?"

"As a very nice, eager, sincere girl," Sister Joan said promptly.

"Untouched?"

"I beg your pardon, Reverend Mother?"

"Would you judge her to be a virgin still?"

"Well, one cannot tell merely from looking," Sister Joan said in bewilderment, "but, yes, I would have guessed she's still a virgin."

"One sees so few truly chaste girls these days," the

Prioress said sadly. "So many women cram all the experience they can into a few years and then present their broken vessels to God. Such a sad waste, don't you think?"

"I really hadn't given it much thought, Reverend Mother," Sister Joan evaded.

"Chastity is the greatest gift we can bring to Our Lady. I entered the religious life at a comparatively late age—twenty-five—but I am proud of the fact that no man had ever laid a finger on me."

Sister Joan bit back a hearty "Bully for you!"

If the other expected some kind of reciprocal confidence she was doomed to disappointment. Past experiences were closed books.

"Well then." The Prioress, having waited a moment, spoke brightly. "Sister David is to be your assistant, so it seems fitting that she should show you the way to your cell. We will meet again at supper which is at seven."

She tugged a plaited bell-cord against the wall and the outer door opened so quickly that it was obvious the bespectacled nun who entered had been waiting for the signal.

"Sister David, this is Sister Joan who will be taking over at the school," the Prioress said.

"Oh, that will be a great relief, Reverend Mother." Sister David gave a long sigh of pure pleasure. "Some of the pupils are so rough and disobedient that I cannot handle them."

"You mustn't frighten Sister Joan away," the Prioress said, smilingly. "Sister David has always had difficulties with maintaining discipline, haven't you, Sister?"

"I wasn't trained to deal with gypsies," Sister David said, a trace of sulkiness behind her glinting spectacles.

"We must all learn to adapt, Sister David. Now run

along and take Sister Joan with you." Sister Joan was not altogether happy about the "Run along," which smacked of the sort of patronising way in which those in authority sometimes treated their nuns. Sister David, however, giggled as if in obedience to the twitching of a string.

As they went through the antechamber and began to ascend a handsome staircase in the Jacobean style they passed Veronica standing shyly at the side of a plump, freckle-faced woman whom Sister Joan took to be Sister Hilaria. A thin ribbon of purple on one sleeve showed that she too had been a Prioress at some time though she had been referred to as Sister instead of the Mother to which her previous position entitled her.

Before she could ask she was set straight.

"That is Mother Emmanuel. She always likes to introduce the new novices. Sister Hilaria is inclined to become rapt in prayer so Mother Emmanuel is a great help in this respect. Our cells are here in the north wing. The house is very logically set out. The chapel is in the other wing with some storerooms above. The dining and recreation rooms are above the public parlour in the main wing and the kitchen and infirmary are underneath our cells."

"I'm sure that I will find my way around quite easily," Sister Joan said soothingly as they reached the top of the staircase and the other paused for breath.

"Oh, I am sure you will," Sister David said fervently. "We are a very happy Community here, all pulling together in the hidden life of Nazareth so to speak. This is your cell."

Rather to Sister Joan's relief the narrow slip of a room with one wall of hardboard to denote that it was only half of the original chamber was like every cell she had ever seen, its walls whitewashed, its floor covered with brown linoleum, a plain wooden cross dark against the whiteness, a narrow bed, a basin and ewer on the floor, a shelf for books, and hooks for her clothes behind a plastic curtain. Her suitcase stood on the floor. "I'll leave you to wash your hands and unpack," Sister David said. "I do hope you will be happy with us. Reverend Mother Ann is a splendid Superior, perfectly splendid."

Unusual certainly, Sister Joan thought, sitting down on the edge of the bed as the door closed softly behind the other nun. Never in her life, even before entering the religious life, had she met a nun whose nails were varnished pale pink and whose habit was scented with lavender.

THREE

✠ ✠ ✠

Five years earlier, Sister Joan had entered the refectory of the convent where she had been accepted to do her novitiate and been faced by what had seemed like a sea of strange faces turned towards her. She had something of that same feeling this evening when, shepherded by Sister David who had come to collect her, she entered the huge chamber where the rest of the Community were already seated, the professed nuns at one long table with the Prioress at the head, the novices at a side table. Double doors at the far end of the room led, she assumed, into the recreation room.

The whole of this upper floor must originally have been a ballroom in the days when balls were held. The polished floor and pale walls with darker panels where once mirrors had been, the ceiling with its central rosette from which a sparkling chandelier still hung, the long windows shrouded by dark velvet curtains, demanded girls in low-cut gowns, young men eager to sign dance cards, and a Strauss waltz tinkling in the background. Instead there was the Prioress, raising her well modulated voice to say, "Sisters, let us give thanks to Our Lady that Sister Joan has come. She is to take over the teaching at the school, and Sister David, for one, is delighted to see her. Sit down.''

Sister David went to what was apparently her usual place and Sister Joan took the chair remaining, tucking the long white napkin under her chin, crossing herself as a nun further down the table intoned the Grace.

Sister Margaret was serving the food, her plump frame moving with swift lightness from serving-trolley to table. Sister Felicity stood at the lectern, preparing to read the notices. When she began Sister Joan was pleased to hear her clear voice. All too often the sister who read the notices mumbled so that one missed half of the information, or rushed through it, no doubt eager to get to her own supper. Sister Felicity read at a measured pace with emphasis in the right places.

''Mr. Grant Tarquin has given permission for the Solstice Festival to be held in the north meadow as was done last year. He does request that we make sure we don't allow the children to leave any litter around. Sister Clare from our Amsterdam House has been appointed as Prioress in place of Mother Grete who has been called to the Mission Fields in Sudan. In view of the political situation in central Africa your prayers are particularly sought. As Sister Joan will be working full-time at the school she is excused garden duty but Sister David is reminded that when she is not required to assist at the school she must take her turn at the weeding.''

Sister Joan, scooping up excellent vegetable stew, wondered if there was something wrong with her hearing. She could have sworn that Sister Felicity had spoken of the Solstice Festival. Nobody else seemed to have noticed anything amiss. Apart from the Prioress only nine sisters were ranged down both sides of the main table. The three oldest nuns would eat in the infirmary, she supposed. The necessity of keeping her eyes on her plate made it quite impossible to study each individual face. Lifting them briefly she was surprised to see a place laid opposite her with nobody sitting in the chair.

Her swift upward look had been noted. As Sister Felicity came to the end of the notices the Prioress said,

"I can see that Sister Joan has noticed our empty place. Can you guess for whom it is intended, Sister?"

"No, Reverend Mother Ann."

Plates of toasted cheese were being handed down the table.

"It does not occur to you that one day Our Blessed Lady may wish to share our meal?"

Sister Joan forgot about custody of the eyes and frankly stared.

"She has visited other convents," the Prioress said. "You will remember how when Saint Teresa of Spain was delayed by a rapture her place was taken by the Blessed Virgin Who came to take her place at evening prayers. You will remember how Saint Catherine Laboure was interviewed by the Blessed Mother in the chapel of her convent in the Rue du Bac. We cannot claim to harbour any potential saints here, but who knows whom Our Lady will deign to honour."

Sister Joan had a sudden, irreverent picture of the Holy Virgin chewing a slice of cheese on toast and sternly forbade herself to grin. Some comment was evidently required however. She said, trying to sound calm and sweet,

"Those are wonderful stories, Reverend Mother Ann."

"More than stories, Sister Joan." The voice was gently reproachful. "Of course it may never happen, but we lay a place as a symbol that She will always be welcome among us." Silence descended. The toasted cheese was succeeded by baked apples and cups of weak coffee. The food was good anyway, Sister Joan thought with relief. She had never believed that badly cooked, inadequate meals heightened one's religious impulses.

There was a concerted rustle as the Community rose for the short prayer after a meal. The four novices were being shepherded away by Sister Hilaria. She was the Novice Mistress who got lost in prayer and had to be helped out by Mother Emmanuel, Sister Joan reminded herself. Presumably she had eaten sufficient to earth herself since Mother Emmanuel was heading towards the recreation room. The two lay sisters had begun to clear away.

"Shall we go to recreation?" Sister David said, popping up at her side like a short-sighted rabbit appearing out of a hat. With her twitchy nose and slightly protruding teeth she did indeed look faintly rabbit-like.

The double doors at the end of the room had been opened and led, Sister Joan had guessed, into another huge apartment with chairs set ready in a semi-circle and a long table piled with work baskets.

"I understand that you worked at embroidered objects before," the Prioress said from her place in the centre of the semi-circle.

"Yes, Reverend Mother Ann."

Tapestries that would cover kneeling-mats and pew cushions, flower pictures to be sold at Christmas bazaars, now and then a stole or a cope for a newly ordained priest.

"Tonight you are excused from working during recreation," the Prioress said. "If you wish to spend part of this period in exploration of the House or quiet prayers in the chapel you are free to excuse yourself."

"Thank you, Reverend Mother."

For the moment she was content to sit at the end of the arc of chairs, her gaze turned towards the other nuns, now settling themselves with their knitting and sewing. The Prioress was not working. Her hands with their pink varnished nails were folded in the lap of her purple habit; her dark eyes surveyed the sisters with unremitting sweetness. At her left loomed the large, freckled face and hands of Mother Emmanuel knitting with a ball of violent green wool what looked like a scarf for the neck of some hapless priest. At her other side Sister David was darning a pair of black cotton stockings. Sister Joan had feared that Sister David might prove to be limpet-like, but she had obviously done her an injustice.

"The rest of us had better introduce ourselves," the Prioress said, when all were seated. "Now whom have you not yet met? Ah, Sister Dorothy is our librarian." Sister Dorothy looked as if she had been created for the task of librarian, with her rimless spectacles and slightly hunched posture. As the Prioress paused encouragingly she said,

"We have an excellent library here, Sister Joan. Much of it belonged to the Tarquin family and was sold with the house. Each sister is permitted to choose one book per week to keep in her cell and read in her leisure time."

In Sister Joan's experience leisure time didn't total up to more than a twenty-minute period in any one week, but the thought of borrowing a book, of dipping into it at odd moments was attractive.

"Sister Martha is our chief gardener," the Prioress was continuing, nodding towards a thin delicate-looking nun who ducked her head shyly, mumbling something. "Sister Lucy is our choirmistress and sacristan."

Sister Lucy was young and pretty. Sister Joan, catching her triangular smile, was reminded of a sleek little cat who might or might not scratch when stroked.

"Sister Perpetua is our infirmarian and Sister Katherine is in charge of the linen."

It was impossible to distinguish neatly between these

veiled heads and identical habits. Nuns *en masse* had as little individuality as an army. Only in personal conversations away from other listening ears might the individual woman under the habit emerge.

"You have not yet met the older sisters in the infirmary," said Sister Perpetua who, from the whiteness of her skin and the russet tone of her eyebrows, could be assumed to be a redhead. "I hope you will find time to visit them, Sister. They are most interested in any little event that relieves the monotony of their days."

"I hope that my coming won't remind them of their recent loss," Sister Joan said.

"Mother Frances, you mean?" Sister Perpetua's kind crumpled face brightened. "What a truly fine old lady she was. Sharp as a needle to the end. Such a loss to the Community when one like that goes."

"A gain for heaven, Sister Perpetua," Mother Emmanuel said.

There was always someone like Mother Emmanuel in a convent, Sister Joan thought. Before it had been Sister Francis who could be relied upon to provide the religious cliché.

"If heaven is already perfect how can further perfection be added?" Sister Dorothy asked. Behind the rimless spectacles her eyes were intelligent.

"That is a most interesting theological point," the Prioress said. "How would you answer?"

Her dark eyes smiled at Sister Joan.

"Perhaps there are degrees of perfection, Reverend Mother Ann," she said. "A small wine-glass can be as full as a large wine-glass. Saint Teresa of Lisieux made that point to one of her novices."

"It was Saint Teresa's eldest sister, Pauline, who actually made that point to the Little Flower herself when she was a child." Sister Dorothy had a triumphant air.

"You are quite right," said Sister Joan placidly.

"Are we then to extend the boundaries of heaven every time a good person dies?" the Prioress asked. Her tone was playful.

"Only if one is a Fundamentalist," Sister Joan said.

If this was some kind of theological word-game designed to show up her ignorance she didn't feel like playing.

"Sister Mary Concepta has a little stomach-ache today," Sister Perpetua said, with an air of pouring oil on troubled waters.

"Nothing serious, I hope, Sister?" Sister Lucy looked concerned.

"Too many chocolates. Her nephew will insist on sending them and she is not always as scrupulous about sharing them as she might be," said Sister Perpetua.

"The old must be allowed their little selfishnesses," the Prioress said tolerantly.

"I understand that I am actually a replacement for two sisters," Sister Joan glanced around.

"I hope you do not regard yourself as a substitute, Sister Joan," Mother Emmanuel boomed suddenly. "We each have our unique contribution to make."

"I was referring to Sister Sophia," said Sister Joan. "She also died, did she not?"

Mother Emmanuel dropped a stitch and clicked her tongue in annoyance.

"You will have your work cut out to maintain her standards," the Prioress said. "You will all have seen the new novice, Veronica. Did you gain any strong impression?" She looked brightly round the semicircle as she asked the question.

"Most promising, I would say," said Mother Emmanuel. "Polite and modest. Very different from some of today's young girls."

"I too gained a favourable impression," the Prioress nodded. "Chastity has its own perfume." Sister Joan wondered if it was lavender and was shocked at the trend of her own thoughts.

"If I may be excused—?" She began to rise.

"Certainly, Sister Joan." The Prioress nodded pleasantly. "Do you need a guide or do you enjoy exploring by yourself?"

"I was going to the chapel," Sister Joan said.

"Down the stairs and turn left. The plan of the building is very simple. We will see you at Benediction. Father Malone will be coming over."

It was then a conventual benediction without any members of the laity there. Giving the customary bow, receiving the customary "Dominus tecum" she left the recreation-room and walked back through the dining-room. The tables had been cleared, the long white napkins neatly folded. There was no sign of the two lay sisters who, she surmised, would be now enjoying their own supper or perhaps tending to the three old dears in the infirmary.

On the landing she stood for a moment, looking down into the shadowed hall. The familiar convent smell of incense and beeswax permeated the air. The old wood of the balustrade slid like silk under her hand as she descended. On the left an archway led into an antechamber similar to the one where she had waited earlier. This one had a heavy grille along the inner wall. The visitors' parlour would be beyond the grille reached by an outside door.

That had been the most final moment, that clashing down of the grille as she passed from lay life to religious life. Two years before. It seemed longer. She had walked through without looking back knowing that Jacob wouldn't be there. It was a measure of how much she had matured in the two years since that were she to take her final vows and pass beneath the grille again she would not hesitate to glance back with love.

The chapel would be behind the visitors' parlour. A low doorway led her into a narrow many-windowed passage running between the right-hand walls of the two parlours and the right front of the main wing. This part of the house felt older than the rest. She passed a side door through which visitors evidently stepped and saw the glow of the Perpetual Lamp gleaming redly through a half-open door.

The chapel was pre-Elizabethan, she calculated, standing for a few moments by the holy water stoup, feeling as she always felt that mixture of awe and heart-shaking love when she stood in the place where the core of her life was held.

No attempt had been made to modernise the interior. Stone walls and floor, a heavily carved wooden ceiling of a later date than the chapel itself, polished pews and pulpit, black and white kneeling-mats.

Sister Joan slipped into the nearest pew and knelt, back straight, hands echoing the candle flames that streamed upward from the altar. The altar was set in the traditional place against the wall with a large crucifix flanked by candlesticks beneath the veiled Host. Within the altar rail was a low table covered with a white cloth. The scent of spring flowers mingled with the incense. Her beads slid, cool black tears, through her fingers as she began a decade of the rosary.

Crossing herself, letting the chain on which her prayers were strung fall freely from her belt again, she rose, her eyes becoming accustomed to the flickering light.

The chapel was larger than she had thought. No doubt in the old times tenants and servants had worshipped here with the Tarquins. The imagined echoes of their devotions were almost audible.

To the right of the altar was a rood screen, hiding the door into the sacristy where the priest robed and dis-robed, where missals and hymnbooks and boxes of candles were kept. To the left was the smaller Lady altar with its statue of the Holy Virgin, crowned head high, blue painted robe falling in frozen curves of plaster to rose-decorated feet. There were candles lit there too and a bowl of flowers on the step.

"Nothing is wrong in this chapel," thought Sister Joan and she was immediately puzzled as to what might have led her to believe there might be something wrong.

Tiredness played tricks sometimes with the mind. She recalled suddenly how, as a child, waking from a bad dream she had gone into the sitting-room and seen strangers there, people with whom she had nothing to do. She had stood, terrified, on the threshold of the room and then the strange woman by the fire had turned her head and smiled and resolved herself into Mum.

But the Holy Virgin was the Holy Virgin. She wasn't about to turn into someone else while Sister Joan stood there staring at Her.

A slight cough by the door made her jump so violently that she was ashamed when Sister Perpetua said,

"Do forgive me, Sister, I didn't mean to startle you, but I just came from tucking in my old ladies. I promised them that you would see them tomorrow and they look forward to it very much. New faces always stimulate them splendidly."

"I hope I don't stimulate them too much," said Sister Joan.

"Heavens, what a thing to say." In the candlelight Sister Perpetua's reddish eyebrows wriggled furiously up and down on her white forehead. "Would you like to take a short stroll before Benediction starts?"

Sister Joan would have preferred to take it alone but the thought of company was not unpleasant. And this was the infirmarian who had known Mother Frances and might clear up the mystery of that last letter.

They went out through the side door into the rain-sparkled dimness of the May evening. At this end of the land the light stayed longer than in the north. It was not a black but a grey cloak that spread itself over the landscape. From a nearby oak a rook cawed into the air, intent on prey.

"This is the enclosure," Sister Perpetua said, unlatching a high wicker gate and passing through it.

The Order of the Daughters of Compassion was not entirely cloistered as were Orders such as the Carmelites. Any sister who wished to immure herself completely must first receive the unanimous consent of all the Prioresses. In the fifty years since the Order had been founded only two sisters had sealed themselves into a hermit existence.

The dim twilight revealed the kitchen garden with its staked vegetables and borders of herb. A cobbled yard with the outlines of stable and garage diminished the space intended as the exercise area. There were rose bushes and spiky lavender to scent the air and against the farthest wall pear and cherry and walnut spread branches heavy with blossom.

"I love the enclosure," Sister Perpetua said. "Now that summer's on the way my old ladies will be able to come out here and sit."

"Are they very sick?" Sister Joan asked as they passed the winding path.

"Sister Andrew has had breast cancer, but thank God she's in remission at present," Sister Perpetua said. "Sister Mary Concepta suffers from rheumatism. Sister Gabrielle is just old. They're all three old but quite bright still. At least they're finishing their lives with some dignity."

It was one of the benefits of a religious vocation, Sister Joan thought, that no nun ended her days in loneliness living on Welfare. To the last breath the old sister remained an integral part of the Community to which she had dedicated her life.

"You must have been sad to lose Mother Frances," she said aloud. "Reverend Mother Agnes told me that she used to be her Novice Mistress."

"Oh, Mother Frances spoke of her often," Sister Perpetua volunteered. "She remembered all the novices who had passed through her hands, but Reverend Mother Agnes was always special to her. I think she hoped for a visit from her before the end came."

"But she did write, did she not?"

"A few days before her death," Sister Perpetua answered promptly. "She wanted her to visit, you see, but one realises that a Prioress cannot uproot herself at a moment's notice and come dashing down to Cornwall to see an old friend. I think Mother Frances also realised it. Very soon afterwards she lapsed into a coma and died. It was a holy death."

Sister Joan nodded. The holy death was one to be anticipated by any sister who had spent her religious life in the tranquil carrying out of her vows and duties. In such a death soul and body separated gently with little anguish, the soul helped on its homeward flight by the prayers and invocations of the assembled nuns.

"Reverend Mother Agnes would have liked to come," she said.

"She telephoned," Sister Perpetua said. "By then Mother Frances wouldn't have recognised her, I'm afraid. Did you know that originally she was a Sister of Charity?"

"Mother Frances? No, I didn't."

"She entered the religious life when she was twenty-one. When our Order was founded she obtained permission to transfer. She knew our Foundress personally. Think of that."

"I fancy that Marie Van Lowen was quite a woman," Sister Joan said.

"A great sinner who may yet become a saint if Rome agrees. The problem is that in Rome everybody moves at a snail's pace."

Sister Perpetua had unfastened a gate set in the wall and was stepping through. Sister Joan, following, was momentarily stilled by the glinting white crosses that marked the close-cut turf.

"Our convent cemetery," Sister Perpetua said. "We will all lie here one day." There were no more than a dozen crosses, in two neat rows, like children at assembly. Each cross bore name and dates of birth and death. Underneath the mounds the sisters slept, clad in their shrouds, uncoffined according to custom.

Two of the graves were marked not by crosses but by small plaques.

"Mother Frances," Sister Perpetua indicated one. "The cross will be set in a year's time when the earth has settled."

That too was according to custom.

"And the other is Sister Sophia?"

"I have a torch," Sister Perpetua said unexpectedly and switched it on, directly at the engraved plaque.

"Sister Sophia Weldon.
1963–1987"

The engraved letters, white against the black, were square and neat.

"She was very young," Sister Joan said, shocked.

"She had taken her vows three months before," Sister Perpetua said, switching off the torch again.

"What happened?"

"She hanged herself," Sister Perpetua said.

"Hanged herself?" The words made no sense. "But

surely—the announcement of her death—I cannot recall—''

''Reverend Mother Ann did not make the manner of her death public to our other Houses,'' said Sister Perpetua, beginning to walk back to the gate. ''We do not discuss the incident, but I felt it only fair to let you know so that you don't inadvertently say the wrong thing. It was and is a most painful subject.''

Across the enclosure the bell for Benediction began to ring.

FOUR

✠ ✠ ✠

The clanging of the rising-bell woke Sister Joan at five. One of the lay sisters, Sister Felicity she realised as the sleep mists cleared from her brain, was striding past the cells, her voice raised above the ringing.

"Christ is risen."

"Thanks be to God," came in a ragged chorus of voices. A series of soft bumps indicated knees hitting the linoleum.

Sister Joan's knees hit the linoleum with the rest. She had not slept well. The train journey, the unfamiliar surroundings, the questions buzzing in her brain had all conspired to keep her wakeful until the clock had chimed one.

The water in the ewer was cold. She splashed her face and hands, blinked the grittiness out of her eyes, reached for a towel. Five years of practice had made her expert at cleaning her teeth while on her knees. Rising, she stripped off nightgown and mobcap and donned the sensible cotton underwear deemed suitable for a professed sister. Her grey habit was one of two that she possessed, to be worn month and month about so that one could be regularly cleaned.

"I fear that in the old days the odour of sanctity was

43

less than savoury in hot weather,'' Reverend Mother Agnes had said.

This Prioress smelled of lavender, not the faint perfume that might result from her laying her clothes with bags of the flowers in the folds, but the stronger essence that comes from a bottle of cologne.

Sister Joan fastened her belt and pinned her veil, her hands moving competently in the absence of mirrors.

''You look awfully well,'' her parents always said on their twice yearly visits, as if they had expected otherwise.

''You get more like your mum every day,'' her father always commented.

She saw herself therefore not in mirrors but in memories of the photographs of her mother she had seen down through the years, the slim figure, the rosy cheeks and vivid blue eyes, the upturned nose and the mouth that quirked upwards in amusement at everything strange and spare.

The nuns were emerging from their cells, walking with folded hands and lowered eyelids along the corridor and down the main stairs to the lower passage that led to the chapel. Lamps burned at intervals to remind them that dawn was not yet come. There would be private devotions and meditation until six thirty when the priest would arrive to offer Mass. On the previous evening she had been too shaken by Sister Perpetua's revelation to notice more than that Father Malone was small and elderly with the expected accents of County Cork in his voice.

In the chapel she conscientiously ploughed through five decades of the rosary and then, her Missal open at the Office of the day, composed in her mind the letter she would later write to Reverend Mother Agnes and slip into a postbox without first submitting it for inspection.

"In the Name of Our Blessed Lord.

"Dear Reverend Mother Agnes,

"Knowing your anxiety in this matter I am writing at once, first to inform you of our comfortable journey and safe arrival at the Cornwall House. We were met at the station by Sister Felicity, one of the lay sisters, and warmly welcomed. This is a mansion house, built in varying styles and at varying periods added to though not always happily from an aesthetic viewpoint.

"The only information of any consequence that I have yet discovered is that Sister Sophia who taught in the school here until her death six months ago took her own life, a circumstance not advertised to the other Houses of our Order. She was twenty-four years old and had been professed for only three months. This tragedy is not discussed among the sisters but the infirmarian, Sister Perpetua, confided it to me.

"I am also told by Sister Perpetua that Mother Frances was deeply respected here and was in command of her faculties almost to the end.

"Reverend Mother Ann is a charming and cultured woman who is obviously well liked by the sisters. The atmosphere here is congenial. I begin my teaching duties tomorrow and hope that I can carry them out to the satisfaction of all.

"Please convey my love to the other sisters and to yourself,

"Your loving daughter in Christ,
"Sister Joan."

To mention the pink nail polish and the scented habit smacked of pettiness. Even the most religious of nuns occasionally flouted small rules and the Prioress of each House had, within her sphere, considerable latitude.

The letter written in her mind she turned her attention back to her devotions. To be perfectly recollected during these daily devotions was a goal to be aimed at, but she feared it would take years before she could so lose herself in prayer as to be unconscious of the small sounds and shufflings of her companions.

Sister Lucy had risen and gone into the sacristy, presumably to greet Father Malone. Through her linked fingers Sister Joan marked her progress, a trifle self-important in its bustling. The sacristan was responsible for the upkeep of the chapel. This one clearly took pride in her position. Too much pride? And what business was it of hers? Sister Joan closed her eyes firmly and began on a silent Salve Regina.

The bell tinkled and she rose with the rest as Sister Lucy slipped back into her place and Father Malone trotted up to the altar.

When Sister Joan went into the dining-room for the breakfast of coffee, cereal and a piece of fruit to be eaten standing according to custom she saw the priest there, drinking a cup of coffee. The Prioress beckoned her.

"Father Malone, this is our new sister, Joan." She smiled at them both.

"Welcome to Cornwall, Sister." He shook hands, peering at her comically over the tops of his half-moon glasses. "Would this be your first visit to this part of the country then?"

"Yes, Father. I was born in Yorkshire and made my profession at the London House."

"Ah, Yorkshire is a fine county too," he said tolerantly.

"I'm taking over the teaching at the Moor School," she told him. "In place of Sister Sophia, God rest her soul."

"And the souls of all the faithful departed," he said,

sketching a cross in the air. "Ah, that was a sad accident. Poor soul."

"An accident?" She let her voice rise up into a question.

"Sister Sophia fell when we were testing the fire-safety apparatus," the Prioress put in.

"The rope which should have been looped round her arm slipped and tightened about her neck instead. Sister Felicity and I were below watching her descent, and by the time we reached her—a great loss to the Community."

"But now you have a new daughter, Reverend Mother," Father Malone said cheerfully, with an air of drawing a black line under the past. "Also a new recruit, I understand?"

"Veronica Stirling," the Prioress nodded. "A very sweet girl, Father. I have high hopes of her."

"Under your guidance and that of Sister Hilaria she will surely flourish," he said.

"One can only pray to Our Blessed Lady," the Prioress murmured. "The number of vocations decreases in every Order."

"I tell myself that the Good Lord wants quality instead of quantity," said Father Malone, putting down his coffee-cup. "Well, I must be away back to my sinners and saints. I left my new curate to offer the parish mass. Nice boy but ambitious. One year ordained and has his eye on a Bishopric. Sister Joan, you are in good hands here. I wish you luck in your schoolwork. If you need any advice you know where to come."

He trotted out, tying his scarf as he went. A man content in the life he had chosen, Sister Joan said to herself, watching him. The old type of parish priest who knows what theology he has studied in the Seminary and has retained an innocence of outlook that gains the trust of his parishioners.

Turning she caught the flash of amused scorn in the dark eyes of the Prioress, the slight curl of the mobile mouth.

"A pleasant little man," the Prioress said. "His parish is quite widely scattered. In these parts Protestant Nonconformity is still dominant. It will be easier for him now that he has a curate. Go and eat your breakfast, Sister. Perhaps you would like to introduce yourself to our old sisters in the infirmary then. They have been looking forward to seeing a new face."

"Yes, Reverend Mother Ann." Sister Joan hurried to her cooling coffee.

The clock chimed the half-hour. The lamps had been extinguished and a weak ray of sunlight was struggling through the overcast sky.

The quiet ordered routine of the day had begun in earnest. The Prioress was withdrawing to her own quarters with Mother Emmanuel at her heels. Two of the sisters with gardening aprons over their habits went purposefully towards the enclosure. Sister Katherine was glimpsed at the end of a corridor, half buried under a pile of clean sheets. Sister Joan went conscientiously to her cell, picking up brush and wash leather on the way from the cupboard on the landing where other sisters were also taking cleaning materials. One's cell had to be left clean before one began the daily routine. By daylight she could see the upper corridor had three large rooms at each side, five of them split into two cells each. Her own cell was the second on the left. A card slid into a narrow frame on the door read "Sister Joan." Sister David was on one side of her and Sister Katherine on the other. Three cells beyond stood empty with doors opened wide. She guessed that the three old ladies now in the infirmary had previously occupied them. She wondered as she made her bed, emptied slops, ran the wash leather over her window if her cell had been where

Sister Sophia had slept. If so the nun had left no trace of anguish.

"If you're ready, Sister, we can go down to the infirmary," said Sister Perpetua as she came out on to the main landing again. "Reverend Mother Ann says you are to relax today, get to know us better, go over to the school."

It didn't sound much like relaxation but she let it pass, following the other down the stairs and through a door near the back of the hall just beyond the lowest steps of the staircase.

They were underneath the sleeping-quarters, she realised, in a short corridor with a door on the left and a door opposite.

"The kitchen," Sister Perpetua said, nodding towards the latter. "The lay sisters have their cells just beyond it. This is the infirmary and my old ladies."

The room into which she ushered Sister Joan must once have been the servants' hall, with a row of bells still on the wall and the same brown linoleum as had been laid above. There were lockers against one wall with lace-curtained windows above them that looked into the tangled foliage of the green tinted conservatory. Against another wall three beds were placed, but the three old nuns sat in basket chairs at a low table on which there were workboxes.

It was a curious circumstance, thought Sister Joan, as introductions were made, how after years in a system where the expression of the personality had to be sublimated those who grew old in the discipline of the faith became in their last years more strongly individualistic than old ladies in the world. It would have been impossible to mistake Sister Andrew, with the lines of remembered pain etched deeply into her face, for the twisted and delicately made Sister Mary Concepta, while Sister Gabrielle with her hearing-aid and sharp, clever face was different again. Old and sick as they were there was still a vitality burning in them.

"Sit down, Sister Joan." Sister Andrew was evidently spokeswoman for the others. "We have looked forward to seeing you. You're from the London House?"

"I did my novitiate and was professed there," Sister Joan said, pulling up a stool.

"How long have you been in the religious life?" Sister Gabrielle asked, turning up her hearing aid.

"I was professed two years ago, Sister."

"She's just a baby in the Order," Sister Gabrielle said with a little giggle.

"Everybody seems like a baby to me now," Sister Mary Concepta said wistfully. "Would you believe that I am the youngest of these three? Seventy-eight. Sister Andrew is a year older than I am and Sister Gabrielle is—how old are you, Sister?"

"Going on eighty-three as you well know," Sister Andrew said. "You've come to take over the school, haven't you?"

"In place of Sister Sophia," said Sister Joan, deliberately.

Sister Perpetua had gone out and she sat alone with the three veiled figures, the ivory of their skin yellowed, their eyes hooded.

"God rest her soul." Sister Mary Concepta's twisted hand fluttered into a cross. "Such a sad accident."

"What I would like to know," Sister Andrew said, "is what possessed them to test the fire-escape apparatus so late at night?"

"Was it?" Sister Joan looked from one to the other.

"Eleven at night in December if you please," Sister Gabrielle said looking as if it didn't please her. "Dark and wet."

"So wet that any fire would have gone out anyway," Sister Andrew said.

"That apparatus hadn't been tested in years," Sister Mary Concepta added. "Sheer foolish nonsense. Mother Frances said—"

"Mother Frances, God rest her soul, had a vivid imagination," Sister Andrew said.

"What did she say?" Sister Joan looked from one to the other, but the three old faces had closed up.

"Gossip is a bad habit in a nun," Sister Gabrielle said and giggled again. "That was a pun. I was very good at making puns when I was a girl."

"Have you met Father Malone?" Sister Mary Concepta asked.

"This morning after Mass."

"A pious nincompoop," Sister Andrew said with a savage little smile, or it might have been a grimace of pain. No, not pain. Sister Perpetua had said she was in remission.

"Does he come every morning to offer Mass?" Sister Joan asked.

"He wouldn't trust his curate loose inside the convent," Sister Gabrielle said naughtily.

"Don't be so bold, or you will shock Sister Joan," Sister Andrew reproved. "Yes, he comes every morning and on a good day we go to the chapel, but today we are not having a good day. We were far too excited about your coming. You brought a novice with you?"

"Veronica Stirling."

It was unlikely they would get the opportunity to meet Veronica since for the first twelve months the novice was kept segregated from the professed nuns with the exceptions of the Prioress and Novice Mistress. In this case they would presumably have some truck with Mother Emmanuel too since Sister Hilaria was apt to become prayer-bound.

"She will not have to change her name since she already bears the name of a saint," Sister Mary Concepta said.

"Not like Sister Magdalen," Sister Gabrielle said, and was frowned at by her companions.

"It is not etiquette to speak of those who leave us," Sister Andrew said severely.

"Sister Magdalen was the novice who left? Did you meet her then?" Sister Joan asked in surprise.

"She was here for six months," Sister Gabrielle said, evidently bent upon gossip. "She came last September. There was a great deal of influenza in the convent that month and both the lay sisters went down with it, so the novices had to take over some of the duties."

"Including us," said Sister Mary Concepta.

"It was very pleasant to have such bright young things running in and out," Sister Andrew said. "Such good, kind girls."

"And one of them left?"

"A very pretty girl," Sister Mary Concepta said. "Blue eyes and a very delicate complexion. What we used to call a typical English rose."

"Is this Veronica pretty?" Sister Gabrielle asked.

"Very pretty." Sister Joan felt bewilderment creeping over her. She had never heard that the outward appearance of an intending nun mattered one way or the other.

"I have always felt that brides of Christ ought to be beautiful on the outside as well as the inside," Sister Andrew said. "Only think of the many plain spinster types who used to be thrust into convents because they couldn't catch a husband."

"We none of us speak from experience," Sister Gabrielle said archly.

"Such a pity she changed her mind and went away again," Sister Mary Concepta mourned. "We were sure that she had a very genuine vocation. Mother Frances was quite put out when we were told she had left. She had been sure that the child had a future in the Order.''

''Perhaps she was upset by the accident to Sister Sophia,'' Sister Joan suggested.

The three old ladies looked at her and then, almost in concert, shook their heads.

''Sister Sophia died at the beginning of December,'' Sister Andrew said. ''Magdalen didn't leave until the middle of February.''

And she would not have gone round to say goodbye. Anyone who left the novitiate went with no fanfare, but was given her train fare and allowed one brief telephone call if she so wished to her family. The notice of her leaving would be given out to the Community without any reasons being attached. If it took courage to enter the religious life it took twice as much courage to leave.

''You ask a lot of questions,'' Sister Gabrielle said with a sharp look.

''I was interested,'' Sister Joan said hastily. ''In convents things always seem to me to go along in exactly the same manner.''

''If this is only the second convent you've ever been in then you haven't much basis for comparison!'' said Sister Andrew with the air of one scoring a point.

''You're right, Sister. I talk a lot of nonsense sometimes,'' said Sister Joan. ''And here is Sister Perpetua to remind me that I have other duties.''

Rising as Sister Perpetua entered, she continued cheerfully,

''I'm afraid I am a sad disappointment to the sisters. I am a mere baby in the Order.'' Sister Joan spoke lightly as she rose.

''We are very glad to have you with us nevertheless,'' Sister Andrew said as if she were smoothing over a social gaffe. ''I hope you will come again to visit.''

"We are always at home," Sister Gabrielle added with her high giggle.

"Wonderful, aren't they?" Sister Perpetua said as they went out. "I am very fond of my old ladies."

"Sister, do you have a few moments to spare?" Sister Joan said abruptly.

"I'm going to pick some mint from the garden," Sister Perpetua said. "Sister Mary Concepta fancies that mint tea helps her rheumatic condition. It does not, of course, but it does no harm."

They passed through a side door and were next to the stable. Sister Joan would have liked to go in and make the acquaintance of the horse she would be riding to and from the school but she would do that later. For now she walked with her companion to where borders of herbs confined the vegetable beds.

"Sister Martha is always happy when someone picks her mint," the other said. "She complains that it spreads everywhere."

"Sister, you told me that Sister Sophia killed herself," Sister Joan said, having decided to pounce without warning. "Reverend Mother Prioress told me it was an accident."

The pounce had no effect. Sister Perpetua merely said calmly;

"Well, she would, wouldn't she?"

"Then what makes you think—?"

"Nobody in their senses has a fire drill with only three people present at eleven at night."

"I was told she was testing the apparatus."

"Testing it or whatever—it makes no difference. When you test equipment you do it in daylight."

"Was it faulty?"

"Oh, completely inadequate," Sister Perpetua said, kneeling to snip the mint. "More risky to use that than to take one's chances with a fire, I would imagine."

"Then surely—?"

"Sister Sophia was worried about something," Sister Perpetua said, still cutting the herbs. "She wasn't sleeping well and she came to see if I could give her something. Not that I have any medical training but I've been infirmarian for the last twelve years and my knowledge is fairly extensive. Used in the right quantities herbs are beneficial and gentle in their effects. Anyway I gave her some herbal tea and she went away again."

"Did she say she was worried?" Sister Joan persisted. "There can be other reasons for not sleeping."

"She said she had something to think over," Sister Perpetua said. "Look, I knew Sister Sophia. She was a very practical, sensible young woman. Her vocation was very strong. Sister Hilaria told us she was the most promising of the novices. When she made her final profession she was radiant, Sister. She was where she wanted to be. That was last September. There was an outbreak of influenza shortly afterwards and most of the sisters went down with it. The novices had to help out and Sister Sophia helped out too. Neither she nor I succumbed and she used to come over to the infirmary when she had finished her school work and give me a hand there. Anyway I suppose I was so busy that I didn't notice when she began to change."

"In what way?" Sister Joan had also crouched down. The scent of the mint was exquisite.

"She lost her radiance," Sister Perpetua said, her voice low. "Oh, we all come down to earth once the ordinary routine of the religious life closes about us. But we still retain some part of that—ecstasy that carried us into a convent in the first place. Sister Sophia didn't. She was suddenly very quiet and yet, at the same time, restless and irritable. It was completely unlike her. I didn't press her however. I gave her the herb tea and she went away. A few days later she died.''

"Were you there?"

Sister Perpetua shook her head.

"I was in my cell. Sister Felicity came and woke me up. She said there had been an accident. She and the Prioress were returning from late meditation in the chapel and were taking a stroll round the entire building when they saw Sister Sophia hanging out of the window of her cell. I went at once and helped Sister Felicity to haul her back through the window. The Prioress had hoped that being infirmarian I might be able to help her, revive her, but it was far too late. The fall had hanged her instantly.''

"But surely the police were called?"

"There was no note," Sister Perpetua said. "Nobody else seemed to have noticed she was depressed or having difficulty sleeping. Reverend Mother Ann told us that Sister Sophia had been examining the fire-escape apparatus and complaining that it was out of date. She was quite sure that she had taken it into her head to test the thing.''

"Surely the police were called?"

"Of course. Also the local doctor. Reverend Mother Ann told them there had been a test made of the apparatus and that Sister Sophia had fallen.''

"She lied," Sister Joan said bluntly.

"She told Sister Felicity and me that she wanted to protect Sister Sophia's reputation. It would have hurt her family terribly and prevented her burial in consecrated ground. She felt no good could be served by telling the exact truth.''

"Was there an inquest?"

Sister Perpetua nodded, rising somewhat stiffly from her knees.

"And?"

"Death by Misadventure. The Coroner added a rider about the foolishness of testing faulty equipment without an expert present. I must go back to my ladies."

"Sister, why are you telling me all this?" Sister Joan caught at the edge of the other's habit. "Why are you telling a complete stranger?"

"Mother Frances told me that a sister would be coming—that was no news since Sister Sophia had to be replaced, but Mother Frances said the new sister would bring a breath of fresh air into the convent."

"Did Mother Frances know—?"

"No indeed." Sister Perpetua looked startled. "She was a shrewd old lady though. Right to the end she was very shrewd. And anyway—" She hesitated, the reddish eyebrows working up and down as if each one had an independent life of its own.

"Anyway?"

"Look, I never was a mystic or a dreamer," said Sister Perpetua. "I've always been down-to-earth, practical. I don't imagine things, Sister. But I can feel evil here. Don't laugh but I can feel evil all round me. I had to tell someone, that's all."

FIVE

✠ ✠ ✠

"I do feel that I ought to come with you," Sister David had fretted, "but I promised Sister Martha that I'd get the peas and beans staked. It is a task that requires two people. Of course she could ask—"

"I wouldn't dream of putting anyone to any inconvenience," Sister Joan said firmly. "I am perfectly capable of riding back along the track and finding the school. Sister Felicity pointed it out yesterday."

"Well, if you're sure," Sister David said doubtfully. "Here are the keys. The timetable is on the wall there and the books and registers are in the desk and the cupboards."

"I'm sure I'll find them. Thank you, Sister." Sister Joan had escaped thankfully, walking rapidly to the stable before the other could protest further.

Now, mounted on Lilith's broad back, she trotted through the open gates with a sense of freedom.

"You will never stand being locked up for the rest of your life," Jacob had scoffed, his eyes hiding hurt. "You'll get claustrophobia."

"I'll get over claustrophobia," she had retorted.

The moor stretched away to the horizon at both sides of the wide white-pebbled track. The rain had held off so far but parts of the moor were a dark and sodden brown. There were patches of paler greener grass starred with wild flowers with clumps of blackberry and whinberry and wild gooseberry to trail spiked branches over the turf. Here and there the low ground dipped lower into a narrow valley of bracken. Over the whole brooded an air of waiting calm. This moor, she reflected, sitting easy in the saddle and letting the mare pick her own way, was unlike the Yorkshire moors where she had spent her childhood. Those moors had been steep and windswept with drystone walls to separate the tiny fields from the common land. This landscape was deceptively mild. She suspected granite beneath its placid aspect.

While she was at the school she would write her letter to Reverend Mother Agnes. It would be longer than the one she had composed early that morning. Now she had been virtually appealed to by another sister who felt instinctively that all was not well. And there had been a cover-up which might or might not have been devised to protect Sister Sophia's posthumous reputation.

The low building behind the wall was visible for a fair distance before she actually reached the gate. She dismounted and tethered the mare to the lower branch of a thorn tree that grew outside the wall. There were no other trees save that one and the school building seemed as deeply rooted as the thorn, its walls of grey stone, its roof of dark slate. The building was in good repair, the key sliding easily into a well oiled lock.

She stepped into a small hallway with doors to left and right. The left-hand door revealed when opened a large cloakroom with pegs and hooks and four toilets, two of them with low seats presumably for tiny children. There were tiles on the floor and half way up the walls and a shallow trough for wet boots.

The schoolroom was on the right. It was a large room

with a swivel blackboard at one end and about fourteen flat-topped desks and chairs. There were windows at front and back with baize-covered boards fixed between them. On the boards were pinned drawings clearly executed by the children. She stepped closer to take a look, her mouth twitching as her eye fell on stick-legged beings intended to represent families. One child had drawn her father, a taller, thicker figure than anyone else in the drawing, and then crossed it out with savage black strokes. Did that mean Daddy was dead or that Daddy was hated? She moved on to a more cheerful picture, with an orange-haired mother and father hanging up stars and a Merry Christmas printed lopsidedly across the bottom.

The cupboards behind the blackboards contained piles of exercise books and textbooks, boxes of pencils and crayons, rubbers and sharpeners. There was nothing personal here at all. She had scarcely expected to find anything after six months. All of Sister Sophia's things would have been cleared away after her death. There would be nothing to give a clue to her personality.

The teacher's desk was at a slight angle giving a bird's-eye view of all the desks. It was a high, flat-topped desk with a high-legged chair behind it on which Sister Joan wriggled herself with some difficulty. From this vantage point she would be looking down at her pupils, a position that had its disadvantages as well as its advantages. Whoever had ordered the furniture had not relied entirely on the nun's habit to inspire respect and obedience. She used the smaller of the two keys that Sister David had given her to unlock the desk, folding back the lid to reveal the register with what looked like a floating population of pupils when she turned the pages. There was nothing else in the desk save some pens and a flat box of watercolour paints. She lifted the

lid and read. ''Brenda Williams'' on the slip of paper
pasted on the inside. The paints hadn't yet been used.

The timetable was pinned to the wall behind the desk.
She twisted round to look at it, wondering why anyone
had bothered to write it out since every day was the
same as the day before it and the day that came after.

9.00 . . . Prayers.
9.30 . . . Reading.
10.00 . . . Writing.
11.00 . . . Break.
11.15 . . . Arithmetic.
12.00 . . . Drawing.

It ended there. Presumably the children were not expected to return to school in the afternoon. Judging
from the many Absents in the Register she guessed that
some pupils took the morning off too. It seemed a lax
way in which to run a school.

There had been pad and envelopes in the cupboard.
She slid from the high chair and went to get them,
squeezing herself behind one of the smaller desks to
write.

''In the Name of Our Blessed Lord.
''Dear Reverend Mother Agnes,

''I am writing this in the schoolhouse where I
shall be teaching every morning. We had a safe and
uneventful journey down into Cornwall and were
met by Sister Felicity, one of the lay sisters, the
other being Sister Margaret.

''The Cornwall House is large and belonged
originally to the local squire which accounts for its
being a curious mixture of styles added to over the
centuries. There is a rather beautiful and ancient

private chapel to which the parish priest, Father
Malone, comes to offer Mass for the sisters.

"I received a most pleasant welcome which
makes me hesitate before informing you that the
late Mother Frances had, I believe, some reason
for her disquiet. The death of Sister Sophia last
December which was attributed to accident was in
fact suicide. The infirmarian, Sister Perpetua, confided to me that Mother Frances could have had no
knowledge of events but she may have suspected
and wished to discuss the matter with you. According to Sister Perpetua who strikes me as a
woman with an active conscience, Sister Sophia
had complained of difficulty sleeping but had not
seemed to be physically ill. Sister Perpetua was
woken at eleven at night by the Prioress and Sister
Felicity who told her they had seen Sister Sophia
hanging out of her cell window. The cord of the
fire-escape apparatus was round her, and the Prioress persuaded the other two to say they had been
testing the apparatus. That was the story given to
the police and a verdict of Misadventure returned.
This you will already know since the notice of Sister Sophia's death will have been circulated round
our Houses. The Prioress took the steps she did in
order to spare the feelings of the family and ensure
that Sister Sophia was buried in consecrated
ground. I must add that I have heard this story only
from Sister Perpetua who felt the need to unburden
herself to someone, and I can see no reason why
she should lie about so serious a matter. My own
feeling, if I may express it, is that no good purpose
would be served by raking over the affair, but naturally you may have a different opinion.

"I know you will be pleased to hear that Mother

Frances was highly respected and that she was very clear in her mind right up to the end.

> "Your loving daughter in Christ,
> "Sister Joan."

Licking down the flap of the envelope and turning it over to write the address on the front she wondered if she ought to have mentioned the nail varnish and lavender perfume, but that seemed petty. Even a prioress was allowed her small vanities. Indeed she thought it quite likely that nobody else had even noticed. Neither had she mentioned Sister Perpetua's remark about evil. It sounded too melodramatic, too much like a remark passed by a slightly hysterical woman.

A step behind her made her jump guiltily, shielding the letter with her hand as she turned round.

"My apologies, Sister. I ought to have knocked or something, but I'm so accustomed to walking in and out that I forget my manners."

For one crazy second before he spoke she thought that Jacob stood there, with his tall, rangy figure, the shock of black hair which continually fell forward into his eye. It was not Jacob, of course. It never would be Jacob again.

"You must be Mr. Tarquin?" She squeezed herself back out of the desk.

"Grant Tarquin. Intelligent of you."

"Not really, Mr. Tarquin. I can see this school was privately endowed and as the Tarquins were the local aristocracy—"

"Whoa, Sister." He put up his hand, displaying white teeth in a broad smile. "My grandfather, who incidentally founded this little school, was never higher in the social scale than a knight and my father lost nearly everything my grandfather had built up. We cannot be regarded as even minor aristocracy, if the term itself isn't out of date. You must be the new teacher.''

''Sister Joan.'' She shook hands, her initial impressions fading. The resemblance to Jacob was only superficial. This man was some years older, in his early forties she calculated, with nothing about him of Jacob's quick, sharp, bitter charm.

''I saw Lilith at the gate,'' he said. ''Did you ride her over?''

''Is she yours? I hope that—''

''I left her at the house, or rather my father did. She's quite an elderly lady. I'm glad she is to be ridden again. Sister Sophia and Sister David preferred to walk.''

''You knew Sister Sophia?''

She had spoken too eagerly. He gave her a slightly puzzled look before replying.

''She taught at the school here during the second year of her novitiate.''

''Surely not.'' Her exclamation was involuntary. The rules for the two years of the novitiate had been sternly laid down by the founder of the Order. The first year was spent in strict seclusion, apart from nearly all the professed nuns, concentrating on prayer and hard physical labour with the complete crushing of one's personal will in obedience to the higher Will. In the second year the novices were permitted to join in more with the day-to-day activities of the professed nuns, but under no circumstances did they accept work outside the convent.

''It is unusual, I believe,'' he said calmly. ''However Mother Frances had really grown too old to cope here any longer and Sister David is not fully qualified, so Sister Sophia was given dispensation to work at the school before she was fully professed.''

Sister Joan hadn't realised that Mother Frances had taught here. It would have been logical for her to have remained as Novice Mistress surely, but perhaps she herself had wanted a change. And then she had grown too old and Sister Sophia had been released from the strict discipline of the Novitiate in order to help Sister David.

"You sound as if you are well versed in conventual routine," she said, smiling.

"Would you believe that I once spent a year in a Seminary?" he returned.

"Really?"

"Yes, really. I had a wide idea that I might become a priest. The Tarquins have always been Catholic though most local people are strongly Protestant. I fancied myself as the first Cardinal in the family."

"May I ask what happened?"

"I discovered that I liked girls too much," he said ruefully.

"As good a reason as I ever heard for leaving a Seminary," she agreed.

"My father had just sold off the old homestead and he died soon afterwards. I went into the Stock Exchange and did reasonably well, so I decided to come home again. Built a new house on the outskirts of town, not as grand as the one that is now the convent but much more modern. However I've kept up my association with the Order and with the school here."

"It's a very nice school," she said cautiously. "I suppose it will be all right if I go ahead and rearrange some of the desks?"

"You're the school teacher," he said easily. "I merely pay the bills with a grant from the Council. Did the Prioress tell you that your pupils will frequently be away?"

"I had a look through the register," she said wryly.

"Most of the children bus into Bodmin these days, but a few prefer to start here and transfer to the Elementary School later on. Some of them are the children of the Romanies who camp out on the moor. They still come and go with the seasons. Then there are sheep farmers round here, and their children come to the school.''

''It will be a challenge,'' she said.

''Aren't all children?'' He cocked a black eyebrow at her.

''That's what makes them interesting. Do you have children of your own?''

She was unprepared for the grief that flashed across his face. For a moment his mask of polite indifference was stripped bare to reveal something quivering and raw, as near great rage as sorrow.

''I'm a widower,'' he said. ''No children.''

''I'm sorry. I didn't mean to pry,'' she said carefully.

''You did not,'' he said in the same abrupt way. ''My wife died ten years ago. She was the only woman I ever loved or ever shall love. Does that sound dramatic? It is the literal truth.''

''Such feelings do exist, I know,'' she said quietly.

''If you imagine that I'm going into the Jewish equivalent of a monastery you're vastly mistaken,'' Jacob had said. ''They don't exist and if they did I'd steer clear. The first duty of a man is to be fruitful and multiply.''

''There are many ways of being fruitful—''

''Not in a convent full of neurotic women.''

''Jacob, I do love you. People of different faiths do get married, working something out, but I can't see myself trotting off to Mass with my children going the other way to the synagogue.''

''They wouldn't be Jews. Judaism is inherited through the female.''

''Is it so important to you?'' She had stepped back a pace, staring at him. ''Is it so important, Jacob?''

''I never thought it would be,'' he'd said.

Her last glimpse of him before she walked away had been rage and grief struggling in his face.

"Sister?" Grant Tarquin was gazing at her.

"I was wool-gathering," she said swiftly.

"I wondered if you had everything you need here. You'll be starting teaching tomorrow morning, won't you?"

"Apparently mornings only," she said, glancing at the timetable.

"I have a feeling you'll be exhausted by lunchtime," he said.

"Well, it's true that I haven't taught for five years," she admitted.

Nor stood talking to a man, she realised. She had expected to feel awkward but she felt completely at ease. That was partly due to the man himself, who chatted to her much as he might chat with any other woman, neither assuming an over-hearty manner nor backing off as if she might bite, both things she had observed sometimes happened when a man was faced with a female who had diverted her sexuality into channels where he had no influence.

"If there's anything you need send one of the children over and I'll do what I can to supply it," he said.

"That's very kind of you, Mr. Tarquin. What I propose to do is spend the first few days getting to know the children and finding out what standard they've reached," she said. It was clear there was nothing more to be seen here. After six months she didn't expect there would be. Perhaps there never had been anything, no conveniently forgotten diary or unposted letter to explain why a bright and dedicated young nun had hanged herself from the window of her cell at eleven o'clock one December night. "I'd better be getting back. Wasting time is definitely against the rules," she said, locking the desk, picking up the letter she had written.

"You'll be needing a stamp for that, Sister."

His eye had fallen upon it.

"Just a quick note to my old prioress to let her know that I'm settling in well," she said, hoping her colour hadn't risen.

"I've stamps at home. If you'll trust it to me I'll pop it in the mailbox tomorrow."

"That's very kind of you. I have money for the—"

"What's a stamp between friends?" he said, smilingly.

"Well, thank you."

Handing over the letter she waited until he was outside, then turned to lock the front door. Doing that gave her an unwarranted but pleasant feeling of ownership. Lilith was cropping the short grass within reach of her tether. She evidently remembered her previous owner, raising her head and giving a soft whinny of pleasure.

"Now you can walk off a little of that weight you've put on, old girl."

Grant Tarquin stepped to her, bringing sugar out of his pocket.

"Why Lilith?" Sister Joan asked, preparing to mount.

"Adam's first wife." He showed his white teeth in a boyish grin that lifted the years from his face. "You wouldn't think it to look at her but this placid old lady was once exceedingly skittish. According to the legend Adam's first wife led him such a merry dance that he begged God for a replacement. However this particular Lilith has certainly mellowed in her old age. Nice meeting you, Sister Joan. Give my regards to Reverend Mother Ann, will you?"

He nodded and strode off, becoming more like Jacob again as he diminished into the distance.

SIX

✠ ✠ ✠

"Sister David tells me that you have chosen to go alone to the school this morning." Reverend Mother Ann had a faint note of reproach in her voice.

"Yes, Reverend Mother." Instinctively Sister Joan raised her chin in a gesture her family would have called fighting Yorkshire.

"May I ask why? Sister David is your assistant."

"I know, Reverend Mother, and I'm sure she will be the greatest help, but I don't want the children to get the impression that I'm shielded by her skirts so to speak. I hope to establish my authority on its own merits."

"You sound as if you were going forth to do battle instead of teaching at a very obscure little school."

The smile and voice were ice cream.

"If I were more confident then I'd take Sister David along with me," Sister Joan confessed.

"I can see that you seek always to challenge yourself." The voice and smile were warmer. "Run along then, Sister. Or ride along, should I say?"

The slim hand was raised and the Prioress turned, graceful in her purple habit, to speak to Sister Katherine.

Saddling Lilith Sister Joan felt the small surge of independence she had felt the day before. She frowned slightly, reminding herself that she was still under strict obedience, that if there was ever conflict between her teaching and the religious life the latter must be served first.

Nevertheless she led Lilith out of the stable with a jaunty step. Sister Hilaria was just crossing the yard, a neat little pile of black books in her hands. Sister Joan recognised the books. Every novice was given one in which a daily examination of conscience had to be written down and shown every week to the Novice Mistress. Her own, she recalled, had been crammed with trivialities with the real struggles left out.

"Good morning, Sister!" She raised her voice slightly.

Sister Hilaria paused, looking round vaguely, then said as her gaze lighted on the other, "Were you the one who said Good morning?"

"No, it was the horse," Sister Joan said flippantly.

"With Lilith that would not surprise me." Sister Hilaria smiled. "Such a pity she is not a donkey."

"I beg your pardon, Sister?"

"If she could speak," Sister Hilaria said, coming forward to stroke the velvety nose, "she might tell us many things, eh, Sister Joan?"

"Might she?" Sister Joan echoed in bewilderment.

Sister Hilaria's slightly prominent grey eyes turned towards her. Her features were fine-drawn and delicate, the hands that now took a firmer grasp of the books surprisingly large.

"You are going to teach in the school this morning?" she asked.

"This morning and every morning, provided any of the pupils turn up," Sister Joan said cheerfully. "Sister,

I really ought not to ask but is Veronica Stirling settling down? I travelled down with her on Saturday."

"Oh, she will be quite perfect," Sister Hilaria said, a smile touching her mouth. "Not as perfect as Sister Magdalen, of course, but one cannot hope to find two Magdalens in one convent."

"But she left, didn't she?" Sister Joan said.

"I wish I knew why," Sister Hilaria said wistfully. "If she had come to me and confided any problems she had—but she never seemed to have any problems. She was so happy, so full of enthusiasm. Mother Emmanuel says that occasionally a novice will take it into her head to leave, but Sister Magdalen gave no indication, none at all. You have not been to the Novitiate here, of course, since it is out of bounds to the professed, but it is a most comfortable nest for my four little chicks."

"It isn't part of the main house?"

"There is a small dower cottage at the other side of the old tennis court," Sister Hilaria told her. "We use that as the Novitiate. Mother Emmanuel and I have our sleeping-quarters there, but really they are all good girls, requiring little supervision. I was on my way somewhere?"

"With the Conscience books," Sister Joan reminded her.

"Ah, yes, so I was," Sister Hilaria said, looking at the small pile of books as if she had never seen them before and couldn't imagine why she was carrying them. "Good morning, Sister Joan. If I don't hurry Mother Emmanuel will scold."

But Sister Hilaria as Novice Mistress ranked ahead of a former prioress, Sister Joan thought, mounting up thoughtfully. It might be a case of a woman of strong character who dominated a weaker character, but it was Sister Hilaria whom the Prioress had appointed as Novice Mistress.

"Any nun who sets out to train novices must combine firmness with common sense and find exactly the right balance between devotion and practicalities," Reverend Mother Agnes had said.

Judged by those criteria Sister Hilaria was surely wildly unsuitable. Sister Joan reminded herself sharply that the other probably had hidden qualities that fitted her for the task and rode round to the front of the building with her mind fixed firmly on the morning ahead.

Unlocking the school door she drew a deep breath and consciously straightened her back. The neat fob watch pinned to the bodice of her habit informed her that it was fifteen minutes to nine. She wondered how many parents bustling their children off to school realised that the teacher had already been up four hours.

There was a large, old-fashioned bell hanging in the porch. She stepped out and rang it vigorously. A few minutes later a pick-up truck disgorged half a dozen chattering children. The driver, a man in overalls with straw-coloured hair, was obviously one of the fathers taking his turn in the roster. The truck was followed by a pony trap out of which tumbled three children whose neckerchiefs and hoop rings betokened the Romany.

As two other children mounted on the same pony came trotting down the track she began to anticipate a full attendance. No doubt they had come to have a look at the new teacher, and it depended on the impression she made as to how many returned regularly. It was, she thought, ushering in one pigtailed child, a challenge.

By the time break came she was beginning to wonder why she had ever decided to teach in the first place. Probably because she wasn't gifted enough to make a living from her art. The twelve children who had finally drifted in were split into two distinct camps. There were the farm children, their accents so broad that she had difficulty in understanding everything they said, who sat stolidly and listened without saying very much, and there was the smaller, more vociferous, group of gypsy and travelling children who were more lively but also more restless, constantly interrupting, shoving one another, their eyes bright as squirrels.

At least she had made some kind of start, she consoled herself, watching them run out to play, both groups still separate. She had placed the desks in a wide semicircle and had spent most of the time on her feet instead of on the high chair. She had taken the names for the register, found out the standards they had attained in reading, writing and counting, and now silently blessed Sister Margaret who had given her a flask of coffee and a couple of apples at breakfast time.

She took them out into the fresh air, perching herself on the low wall as she munched and drank. The children, she hoped, would come back when she rang the bell again. For the moment she enjoyed the peace.

A young man was striding along the track. A hiker, she guessed, noting the thick-soled boots, the windcheater and backpack. Certainly not handsome, she thought as he came within view, but athletic and tough with wind-roughened fair skin and reddish hair that curled defiantly despite the aggressively short cut. He caught sight of her, hesitated, then veered in her direction.

"Good morning."

His tone threw doubt on the statement. It was belligerent and the blue eyes meeting hers were wary.

"Good morning." She answered him pleasantly. "It's a fine day for walking if the rain holds off."

"Been a bad month for rain," he agreed. "You're from the convent?"

"From the Daughters of Compassion, yes. You're from round here?" She had heard the flat vowels of

Derbyshire in his accent and so gave him a questioning look.

"Never been here before," he said tersely. "I've come to see Brenda."

"Brenda?" In the split second she asked the question she saw the box of paints in the big desk, the name pasted inside the lid. "Do you mean Brenda Williams?"

"You'll know her then?"

"No, I don't think so. Would you be referring to Sister Magdalen?"

"Magdalen." He snorted as he let the backpack slide to the ground. "Magdalen, if you please! What's wrong with Brenda?"

"I don't think there has ever been a saint called Brenda," she said pacifically. "Nuns always take the name of a saint unless they are fortunate enough to have been christened with such a name already. I was already Joan when I entered the religious life."

"Do you know Brenda?" he broke in with scant regard for politeness.

"I'm new here so I never met her, Mr—?"

"Johnny Russell," he said abruptly, not holding out his hand. "I've come down to see Brenda and I'm not leaving until I have seen her."

"But she left three months ago, if you are talking about Sister Magdalen," Sister Joan said.

"Left? Transferred to another convent you mean?"

"She left the Order. Novices can leave whenever they choose provided they give one month's notice."

She wondered suddenly if Sister Magdalen had done that.

"That's allowed?" He looked disbelieving.

"Nuns aren't kept against their will, I do assure you," Sister Joan told him. "The keys are on our side of the doors. Look, I have to ring the bell and get the children inside again. Classes finish at twelve thirty, so if you can wait until then—?''

"I'll not be persuaded to change my mind," he said stubbornly, "and what's to stop you telephoning the convent and having her hidden away before I can get there?"

"I can see that you're not a Catholic," she said wryly. "Only a non-Catholic would have such mediaeval notions. There isn't a telephone here, Mr. Russell. Perhaps you'd like to come in and check before I ring the bell? Or perhaps you'd like to ring the bell yourself in case there is some secret signal related to the spiriting away of nuns when young men come calling?"

He had the grace to blush and grin, immediately looking more pleasant.

"I'll wait," he said, and strode off, trailing his backpack over the grass.

Ringing the bell she put Sister Magdalen out of her mind with some difficulty and saw with relief that the children were returning.

For the remaining hour and a quarter she devoted time to getting to know her pupils a little better by encouraging them to stand up in turn and tell her something about themselves. Now that she was becoming accustomed to the accents the children themselves seemed less intimidating. She was relieved to make the acquaintance of the child whose drawing on the wall had obliterated the male figure and discover that Daddy had merely taken off with a local barmaid, leaving very little grief behind. Conscientiously she waited until exactly the half-hour before dismissing them and was inclined to regard the morning as not entirely a failure when one of the travelling children fixed her with soulful dark eyes and announced,

"You'm none so bad, Sister Joan. We'm comin' again tomorrow."

The last of them had barely scampered off towards the approaching pick-up truck when Johnny Russell uncoiled himself from the patch of bracken and marched towards her, the light of renewed battle in his eyes.

"Come into the schoolroom and we can talk," she invited. "I take it that you've come to see Brenda Williams who took the name Magdalen?"

"If you don't know her how come you knew her surname?" he asked suspiciously.

"Is this her box of paints?" She produced it.

"She loved painting," he said, lifting the lid. "Yes, that's her printing. What's it doing here?"

"Well, I'm making an assumption," Sister Joan said cautiously, "but nuns don't have personal possessions, not in theory anyway. Novices are certainly not allowed to retain any personal possessions so she probably handed this in and someone thought it would come in handy at the school. I've only been here a couple of days myself so I'm guessing."

"You said she'd left."

"Three months ago."

"That's not possible," he said flatly. "You're just saying that, to keep me from seeing her."

"Mr. Russell, this may come as a bitter disappointment to you," Sister Joan said in exasperation, "but we have quite sufficient to occupy our minds with the sisters who stay without having to resort to melodramatic devices to keep the ones who want to leave. As far as I know the novice Sister Magdalen left the Order in February."

"But she'd have come home, back to Matlock," he said blankly.

"She didn't?"

"No, she didn't." He sat down abruptly on one of the small desks, scratching his mop of reddish curls.

"Her mum and dad think she's still here. They don't even know I've come."

"I take it that you were her boyfriend?" Sister Joan sat down too.

"Yes, I was, not that there was ever any funny business, if you know what I mean."

"I know what you mean. Go on."

"We live in the same street, went to the same school. Her family's Catholic and mine isn't, but that never mattered much. I wouldn't have minded getting wedded in church and having the children brought up as Catholics, not that we were ever actually engaged, but I made it clear what I wanted and I respected her, Sister Joan."

"I'm sure you did," she said gently.

"So it makes no sense. It never did make any sense."

"Her deciding to become a nun, you mean?"

"After she left school she did a year of Secretarial College," he told her. "And then she came home and it was all different. She was different. She'd got it into her head that she wanted to be a nun. She'd read about some woman, Marie something or other."

"Marie van Lowen, the Dutch woman who founded our Order. She died in Dachau."

"I told her it was a crazy idea and she'd hate it, but she wouldn't listen. She was full of bullshit—oh, begging your pardon."

"Granted. Go on."

"That's it," he said simply. "She insisted and I lost my temper, and she came down here to the convent. That was last September. She never wrote to me or to her parents."

"For the first year a novice is in strict seclusion."

"She said something about that before she left. Anyway I tried to forget her, but the truth is that I can't. I can't forget her and I want to see her one more time to give her the chance to say she made a daft mistake.''

"There are four novices here at the moment,'' Sister Joan told him. ''We are not a large Order like the Benedictines or the Sisters of Mercy. In fact our organisation is slightly different from theirs. We have no Mother General for example. Each Prioress is responsible for her own House of which there are three in England, two in Holland, one in France, and two overseas in the mission field. There is co-operation between the various Houses, of course, a certain amount of movement within the Order to keep the numbers correct, which is why I came to replace a sister—two sisters who died; and a new novice, Sister Veronica, came to take the place of Sister Magdalen who left in February.''

"Then why didn't she go home?'' he said.

"Would her parents have been angry at her leaving?''

He shook his head. "Mr. and Mrs. Williams are good Catholics,'' he said, "but they didn't really want to let her go into the convent. They always approved of me as a boyfriend.''

"How old are you?'' Sister Joan asked gently.

"Twenty-one, I was in a higher class at school than Brenda. I'm working in my dad's shop now. Well, not at this precise time—I'm on a walking-tour in the Lake District.''

"I think you went adrift somewhere or other,'' she said lightly but his face remained sombre.

"She'd have gone home,'' he said. "I know she would.''

"Mr. Russell—look, may I call you Johnny? Would you be willing to trust me for a day or two?''

"Why?'' he asked bluntly.

"Because I'm asking you to trust me,'' she said simply. "I'm new here as I told you, but I'm—perturbed about certain things that have been going on around here. One of the old nuns who died recently was worried too.''

"What things?" he said, still suspicious.

Sister Joan hesitated, aware that gossip about the internal affairs of any religious Order was undesirable.

"When a novice leaves," she said finally, "she must give one month's notice. During that time she must search her heart and conscience, talk over everything with the Novice Mistress or the Prioress because once she does leave she is not allowed to return to the Daughters of Compassion though she may decide to enter one of the other Orders. When she does leave she is given a ticket to wherever she chooses to go, and the money—we call it dowry—that she brought with her. Then her original clothes are returned to her and she leaves quietly, without seeing any of the other sisters. From what I have gathered Sister Magdalen was as happy as a lark. Her Novice Mistress was astonished when she left.''

"Perhaps the Novice Mistress is lying?" Johnny suggested.

"Sister Hilaria is a very holy nun," Sister Joan said severely. "She is something of a mystic. No, she was not lying.''

"Perhaps Brenda ran away?"

"But after giving a month's notice she could have left anyway. Was she the kind of girl who was apt to run away?''

"Brenda was a sensible girl," Johnny said firmly. "The only stupid thing she ever did was to decide to become a nun, and she said she'd thought about that for quite a long time while she was away at Secretarial College.''

"Johnny, is it possible that she met someone else while she was at college?''

"No," he said simply. "She was a straightforward

girl. If she'd met someone else then she'd have told me about him. I wouldn't have liked it, but I'd have put up with it. No, there wasn't anyone else.''

"Have you enough money to stay in the district for a few days?'' Sister Joan asked.

He nodded.

"I want to make some discreet enquiries before doing anything further,'' she said, wondering what on earth to do if her enquiries were fruitless. "Perhaps you could book in at one of the local inns.''

"Don't you think that might be wasting time?'' he said frowningly. "The police ought to be told if she vanished after she left the convent.''

"Give me until tomorrow,'' she said recklessly. "I teach here every morning so you can come over at lunchtime and I'll let you know how things stand. Oh, and be discreet, won't you?''

"I won't say anything,'' he promised. "Sister, what do you think happened to Brenda?''

"Probably nothing at all,'' she answered with an optimism she was far from feeling. "It is possible that she changed her mind about entering the religious life and slipped away without saying anything. She may have gone somewhere to think things over.''

"For three months?''

"I agree that it does seem a long time. Anyway, I'll see what I can find out and you'll be a tourist for a few days.''

"You said that you were worried about one or two things that were happening,'' he detained her to say. "What things?''

"One of the professed sisters died in December,'' Sister Joan said reluctantly. "She was testing some fire-escape apparatus and she apparently fell. It is possible that her death upset Sister Magdalen—your Brenda.''

"Then why did she wait three months before she left?" he asked.

"I don't know. Probably the two events aren't connected."

And perhaps they were, she thought, shooing him ahead of her, locking the door carefully. It would be something to find out if she could.

"Until tomorrow then," she said with professional brightness. "Try not to worry."

Advice she had better start following herself, she resolved, mounting the patient Lilith and trotting away with the persistent Johnny Russell gazing after her.

SEVEN

✠ ✠ ✠

Sister Joan had missed the convent luncheon which didn't matter too greatly since she had eaten the two apples and drained the flask of coffee. Accordingly she made no attempt to hurry Lilith but let her amble down the track. At each side the low moorland stretched, its sombre aspect intensified by the gleams of sunshine that gilded bracken and grass. When she reached the main gates she veered off the laurel-edged drive, trotting across the lawn that curved around the end of the building and became a paved walkway. On her right was the high wall of the enclosure and ahead of her steps leading down to a sunken and grass-grown tennis-court.

The tennis-court brought home to her the full dilapidation of what had once been a prosperous family estate. The posts were still in position but they were thick with rust and the remnants of a net sagged sadly between them, gaping holes adding to the shabby appearance of this court where young men in blazers and girls in pleated dresses with low waists had once flirted and delivered long sweeping lobs and crisp back shots. If she stayed here long enough she would surely hear the echo of their laughter, stilled now by two world wars, the soft slap of the tennis balls against the racquets.

Dismounting she went down the steps and walked across the court to the wicker gate set in an angle of the two further walls. At the other side of the gate a house, somewhat larger than a cottage, stood with lace-curtained windows hiding the rooms within. That must be the Dower House, now the Novitiate, where the four candidates would live in complete seclusion, coming up to the main house only for devotions, except when there were circumstances, like a serious outbreak of influenza, which forced a relaxation of the rules.

One of the lace curtains twitched slightly. Sister Joan bit her lip, unwilling to be caught trespassing, but also unwilling to take flight like a naughty child. A moment later a side door opened and the thick-set figure of Mother Emmanuel emerged.

"Good afternoon, Sister Joan." She greeted the intruder cheerfully. "Having a little wander?"

"I think I strayed too far," Sister Joan said apologetically.

"I don't think the novices will come to much harm if they glimpse a professed nun out of the chapel," said Mother Emmanuel, coming to the gate and lifting the latch.

"I just got back from school," said Sister Joan, and immediately scolded herself for sounding obsequious.

"You missed lunch then?" Mother Emmanuel glanced at her. "If you go to the kitchen Sister Margaret will make you a sandwich. In the religious life it is important you keep up your strength. Did you find the morning exhausting after so long without teaching?"

"Rather like riding a bicycle. One never really loses the knack," said Sister Joan.

"It is rather like riding a bicycle, isn't it?" the other said. "I mean in the religious life, the keeping a balance between the inner and outer world. We are fortunate here in our Prioress. She is bound to be elected for a second term. A true inspiration to all of us. You know I was Prioress here before her?''

''I assumed so.''

''I had two terms of office turn and turn about with Mother Frances. She had come from our Paris House. I believe she was Novice Mistress there.''

''Reverend Mother Ann—'' Sister Joan began.

''She was librarian here. Much of her time has been spent in collecting and transcribing her late father's papers. He was a famous archaeologist, but I dare say you have been told.''

''Yes, indeed. He left a considerable reputation behind him.''

''She travelled with him all over the Near and Middle East before his death. It is my opinion,'' said Mother Emmanuel, ''that she could have had a brilliant academic career herself, but she sacrificed it first to his comforts and then to the religious life.''

''I was talking with Sister Hilaria this morning,'' Sister Joan said, becoming a rifle bored with this recital of the perfections of Reverend Mother Ann. ''She seems a little vague.''

''You are wondering why she was appointed as Novice Mistress,'' Mother Emmanuel said. ''She is a genuine mystic, you know. Her religious experiences have reached a very high level of sanctity, of which she is modestly unaware. However Reverend Mother Ann felt that she required some position of responsibility in order to balance her. Unfortunately she is somewhat distrait at times, which is why I assist her in the task.''

''May I ask how the novices are progressing?'' Sister Joan saw the opening and leapt in.

''Very well on the whole.'' Mother Emmanual looked satisfied. ''Teresa and Rose will be extremely efficient and dedicated members of the Community. Barbara is apt to think too much of her own will rather than the Will of God, but that is a fault from which we all suffer at times. Veronica is a charming girl, very eager and devout. Of course it is a little inconvenient that she entered later than the others. When they move into their second year she will still be in her first. However that is something to be considered later.''

''You have no second-year novices yet?''

''Reverend Mother Prioress decided to streamline everything by accepting novices only every two years, such a practical step to take.''

''You must have been disappointed when Sister Magdalen left so abruptly.''

''Yes indeed. She had seemed very happy with us, but one can never tell. She came to us last September, a few weeks before the others arrived. She would be embarking on her second year now, mingling more with the rest of us.''

''She didn't confide that she intended to go home?''

''Not to me. Did you ever play tennis, Sister? I have often thought that it might be rather jolly to tidy up the court and use it at exercise time. Reverend Mother Ann used to play when she was a girl. I imagine that she would have been very good.''

''I never played,'' said Sister Joan. ''At our school we played hockey.''

''The Prioress played hockey for the County when she was at school,'' Mother Emmanuel said proudly. ''I would love to have seen that. Well, I must get on. I'm glad the teaching wasn't too difficult. You must make good use of Sister David whenever you need her.''

She nodded briskly and strode off. Sister Joan stood staring after her, wondering if either Mother Emmanuel or the Prioress were conscious of the exact feelings of the former for the latter. Probably not in Mother Emmanuel's case. She guessed that the elderly nun had entered the religious life as a very young girl before she had worked her way through that period of getting violent crushes on members of one's own sex. The Prioress, having entered later in life, might well be taking advantage of the other nun's devotion. She debated whether or not to go and ask Sister Margaret for a sandwich and decided not to bother. It was now midafternoon, a period when the sisters were occupied with their work, either in their cells or elsewhere. It was a rule of the Order that each convent be self-supporting. Any money earned at an outside job went into the general fund. It might be interesting to find out who actually worked at what. There would be a list somewhere or other in the library. As she passed, trying to recall if she had been told its location, she spotted Sister Dorothy hunching herself along from the direction of the enclosure.

"Sister Dorothy, is it all right if I have a look round the library?" she greeted the other. "I will have work to mark in the future but today I am still finding my feet."

"It's above the chapel," Sister Dorothy said, pushing her rimless spectacles higher on her snub nose and peering up at the other. "The room Reverend Mother Ann uses used to be the library, but the books were all moved. Come, I'll show you."

She scuttled ahead towards the chapel, dipping into a hasty genuflection before taking a narrow staircase to the storey above. Sister Joan followed, twitching her nose as the unmistakable smell of dust and mould reached her nostrils.

"These are all storerooms." Sister Dorothy jerked her veiled head towards the corridor with its closed doors at each side. "We keep promising ourselves we will clear them out but there is never enough time.

These two rooms were turned into the library however and are in much better condition.''

She opened the nearest door and went in, standing aside with what in a more extroverted woman might have passed for a flourish.

A very creditable attempt had been made to create a traditional library, with a thick carpet muffling the sound of footsteps, sections of wall between the bookshelves papered in dark red, several small tables and chairs equipped with reading lamps. The door at the far end led into a smaller room full of filing cabinets. Long dark curtains were looped back from narrow arched windows and several pieces of rough pottery stood on the sills.

''Those were some of the artefacts that Professor Gillespie brought back from his expeditions,'' Sister Dorothy said. ''Did you want a particular book, Sister?''

''I just wanted to browse,'' Sister Joan said. ''I can borrow one book a week?''

''And renew it when you need to do Sister Joan,'' said the other. ''Just be sure to sign for it in the book here. Now if you'll excuse me I have some cataloguing to do.''

She gave her little, faintly self-important nod and went off into the inner room. Sister Joan walked slowly along the bookcases, pausing here and there to read a title. The Tarquin family had possessed a handsome collection of books, she thought, noting the bindings of calfskin and tooled leather, the sets of Victorian novels and plays, the volumes of *Punch* and *The Spectator*. Theology also held an important place as might be expected in a convent but there were numerous biographies and collections of poetry. One shelf held a number of large illustrated books of Art History. On another shelf *The Golden Bough* elbowed an atlas.

The list of professed nuns hung on the wall in a neat

frame. She paused to read the names, fitting names to faces in her own mind as she did so.

"Reverend Mother Ann, Prioress.
Mother Emmanuel, Secretary and Assistant Novice Mistress.
Sister Hilaria, Novice Mistress."

Those three would not be expected to have any outside job. Her eyes moved on down.

"Sister Dorothy, Librarian.
Sister Perpetua, Infirmarian.
Sister Lucy, Sacristan.
Sister Katherine, Linen and Embroidery.
Sister Martha, Garden.
Sister David, Teacher.
Sister Joan, Teacher."

Since her arrival a new list had been typed out then.

"Sister Mary Concepta.
Sister Andrew.
Sister Gabrielle."

The three old ladies whose only duty was to live out the rest of their lives in peace and join in the activities of the convent when their health allowed.

At the bottom were the two lay sisters,

"Sister Felicity, Transport and Kitchen.
Sister Margaret, Cook."

Apart from Sister David and herself only Sister Katherine was apparently earning any money from an outside source. Either some of the sisters had brought very large dowries or someone was financing the convent generously.

It had nothing to do with her immediate problems. Shrugging slightly she turned aside and went back to her perusal of the books, thinking with amusement that some of the volumes inherited from the Tarquin family were scarcely required reading for nuns. *The Golden Bough* with its carefully detailed accounts of ancient fertility cults would have sent Reverend Mother Agnes's eyebrows shooting skywards.

On the shelf, prominently displayed, were a dozen thick volumes with titles ranging from *Evidence for the Use of the Wheel in Ancient Peru* to *Hittite Influence in the Holy Land*. These had "Laurence Gillespie" scrawled in gold on the spines and a photograph of the author on the back cover. Sister Joan studied the handsome face with the weary eyes and tried to relate that person to the Prioress. Reverend Mother Ann had inherited the dark eyes, the faint, sweet curve of the lips. She wondered if she had loved her father and if his death had sent her into the religious life because she knew she would never find a man to compare.

"Have you found a book, Sister?" Sister Dorothy had returned.

"This one about Peru looks interesting."

"Oh, Professor Gillespie broke new ground in archaeological analysis," Sister Dorothy said, her eyes lighting eagerly behind her spectacles. "He must have been a remarkable man. He died untimely, you might say. Reverend Mother Ann has devoted her leisure to transcribing and collating all the mass of unpublished work he left behind. Perhaps she will agree to its publication one day."

"Maybe I'll take something lighter. I was looking at the list."

"I typed a new one as you have joined us."

''Not many of us seem to have outside jobs. It must make problems in the finances.''

''We are fortunate,'' Sister Dorothy said. ''Reverend Mother Ann brought a considerable inheritance from her late father into the Order and then the Tarquin family has been most generous. It enables us to concentrate more on the contemplative side of things. Which book will you take?''

''I think I'll stick with Jane Austen. *Emma*.''

''I love Jane myself,'' Sister Dorothy said. ''Sign for it in the book. Excuse me, but I must get on.''

She scuttled away again rather like the white rabbit in *Alice in Wonderland*.

Sister Joan picked out the volume and went over to the flat desk where the book that had been indicated to her lay.

Sister Dorothy had gone into the further room again and there was leisure in which to leaf through and find out what her fellow nuns had recently been reading. More particularly to discover what Sister Sophia had borrowed. Turning back the pages to the previous November she ran her finger swiftly down the names. Yes, there in a small neat hand was *Isis in Palestine* by Laurence Gillespie and the name of the borrower, Sister Sophia. Sister Joan turned back the pages, noting that Sister Sophia had been reading her way through the Gillespie volumes. She wondered why. Perhaps she would do better to take one of them rather than *Emma*. Suiting action to thought she replaced *Emma*, took out *Isis in Palestine*, and signed for it.

As she emerged into the corridor the clock chimed the half-hour. At this time secular work was laid away and the nuns gathered for religious instruction and meditation.

''Sister Joan, I found Lilith tethered near the tennis-court so I stabled her for you.'' Little Sister Lucy of the slanting kitten eyes rose from her knees in the chapel as she came down the narrow stairs.

"That was very kind of you, Sister, and quite unforgivable of me to neglect the poor animal," Sister Joan said gratefully.

"I'll not tell," Sister Lucy said with her little triangular smile.

"When is general confession?"

"Not until Friday evening," Sister Lucy told her. "The penances here are very light. Reverend Mother Ann believes the religious life should be a happy and satisfying one."

"If you imagine," Sister Joan's own Novice Mistress had said, "that you will upon taking your perpetual vows enter at once into an existence of perpetual bliss, let me disillusion you forthwith. Being a nun is not automatically a happy situation to be in and your old faults will surface always when you least expect them. Penance is the discipline of the soul, a discipline that must not be carried to extreme, but must be carried out whenever the personal will threatens to overrule the Will of God."

"I will come with you to religious instruction," Sister Lucy said. "We meet in the Prioress's parlour. The room that used to be the library? I told you."

"Yes, you did." Sister Joan hastened her step as the other went rapidly along the narrow corridor and across the hall.

There had been some slight rearrangement of furniture in the parlour, the tapestry-covered sofas having been pushed back and some stools brought in. Reverend Mother Ann however still occupied a comfortable basket chair. Other members of the Community were filing in, save for the old ladies, the lay sisters and Sister Hilaria.

"Are we all present then?" The Prioress looked

around expectantly at the eight attentive faces before her.

"All present and correct, Reverend Mother Ann."

Another moment, Sister Joan thought, and Mother Emmanuel might start saluting.

"As Sister Joan is the newcomer among us," the Prioress said. "I propose to spend a few minutes explaining the purpose of this instruction. Of course it is the custom in each of our Houses that on five days of the week a period of religious instruction is held every afternoon between five thirty and seven. The form this takes is dependent upon the Prioress. For my own part I feel strongly that since Vatican Two a breath of fresh air has blown through our doctrine. Open discussion, even dissension, is the norm instead of the exception. The old certainties are dissolving."

"Oh dear," Sister Joan thought wryly, "we have a raging liberal here." In her limited experience, inside every liberal was a diehard traditionalist.

"Reverend Mother Ann has been examining some of the new ideas now being aired in certain quarters," Mother Emmanuel said. "We have been looking at the possibility of women priests."

"His Holiness has ranged himself on the side of the conventional thinkers, men who do not believe there is any place for the female within the liturgy of the Church save as silent sisters. What is your opinion, Sister Joan?"

The Prioress smiled at her encouragingly. Sister Joan felt a tremor of alarm.

"May I be permitted to listen for a while, Reverend Mother?" she asked. "I am not used to this kind of completely open discussion."

"But you must have some opinion, Sister," Sister Dorothy said. "I noticed you borrowed *Isis in Palestine*."

"One of my late father's must successful books." Reverend Mother Ann looked gratified.

"I fail to see—" Sister Joan hedged.

"Isis was the generic name given to the Mother Goddess of the human race," the Prioress said. "It was my dear father's opinion that Our Lady was in the same tradition, and ought therefore to be worshipped in partnership with Her Spouse."

Mariolatry run mad, Sister Joan thought. She said cautiously,

"I was always taught that worship is given only to the Blessed Trinity and that hyperdulia, great respect, is to be paid to Our Blessed Lady."

"We are in the Age of Aquarius," Sister Lucy said brightly.

"A pertinent point. Women are now coming into their own. My late father was of the opinion that originally all religious ritual was in the hands of the women, but that this was superseded by the patriarchal beliefs and practices of the early Israelites. Now the Goddess is coming into her own again."

With a silent spasm of hysterical laughter Sister Joan wondered if the Bishop was ever invited to one of these sessions. She thought it highly unlikely.

"In ancient times," Mother Emmanuel said, "the prettiest young girls laid their virginity at the service of the Goddess. There is a most interesting passage about that in *Isis In Palestine*, Sister. It explains a great deal."

"Is Veronica pretty and a virgin?" the Prioress had asked.

"Sister Magdalen was very pretty," someone had said.

Sister Joan sat very still, letting the voice of the Prioress slide past her. What was being discussed here was as near to heresy as made no difference. Were the novices being fed this pagan viewpoint? Was that why Sister Magdalen had left so abruptly? Why Sister Sophia had hanged herself?

She slid her eyes along the row, noting expressions and attitudes. Mother Emmanuel was leaning forward slightly, her eyes intent on Reverend Mother Ann, her head nodding frequent agreement. A woman nearing sixty trapped in the emotions of her teenage years. Sister Dorothy sat hunched up, the late afternoon sunlight striking the lenses of her spectacles so that she looked curiously blind and mole-like. Sister Lucy was running her tongue round the inside of her lips like a cat that scents milk or a mouse. Sister David was listening with an expression of such intelligence on her face that Sister Joan wondered if she knew what they were talking about. Sisters Martha and Katherine sat side by side looking blank. At the end of the semicircle Sister Perpetua's hand gripped her crucifix so tightly that the knuckles showed white.

Something about a crucifix. No, a statue. Something about a statue. Her mind groped but failed to bring the image into focus.

She ought to have asked Sister Margaret for a sandwich. Her stomach was growling. Reverend Mother Ann was talking about the Caananites and their worship of Astarte. She had some good points to make, Sister Joan admitted, pressing her hand against her stomach. The link between paganism and Christianity was too seldom explored, but the Prioress seemed to be suggesting that one should regress to the other. Her stomach growled again and Sister David gave a stifled giggle.

"Sister Joan went without her lunch because she was busy at the school," Mother Emmanuel said.

"Sister, you must go at once to the kitchen and ask for something to tide you over until suppertime," Reverend Mother Ann said. "You are excused."

She sounded relieved rather than annoyed to be rid of a disruptive influence in the quality of her audience.

Sister Joan gripped her book, rose obediently and bowed, receiving in return the ice-cream smile.

To the right of the Prioress the last rays of scarlet sun gilded the statue.

Sister Joan must have walked to the door and opened it and passed through because she found herself on the other side of it in the antechamber. She stood, staring at the smooth panels, trying to decide if the Prioress or any of the others were aware that the Madonna in the parlour was an exact copy of the crowned Isis she had once admired in the British Museum. The museum statue had been of dark red marble or porphyry. This one was of smooth pale wood. The splashing red of the falling sun had focused the image in her mind. Quite unbidden there rose up in her mind the entirely unpious question,

"What the hell's going on here?"

EIGHT

✠ ✠ ✠

Though her stomach was still growling Sister Joan turned not in the direction of the kitchen, but in the direction of her cell. Perhaps it was time to have a look at the book she had borrowed.

Isis In Palestine was, as she had surmised, an analysis of the Mother Goddess cult in the Holy Land, written in a fluent but scholarly style that was pleasant to read. Professor Gillespie clearly knew his subject and took a faintly mischievous delight in tracing connections between the worship of Astarte/Isis and the Catholic devotion shown to the Virgin Mary. There were several photographs of many-breasted Dianas and of the professor himself at the sites of various digs. What she failed to find as she skimmed through it was any spark of truly original research. Professor Gillespie leaned fairly heavily on the work of previous investigators, and seldom bothered to credit them with having done the research first. The impression she gleaned was of a man whose undoubted intelligence was derivative rather than initiative and whose personality was a mixture of charm and egotism. She suspected that he had bequeathed those qualities to his daughter. Which did nothing to solve the mysteries of the death of Sister Sophia or the abrupt departure of Sister Magdalen. She would have to find out more about the former. There would be the official notice of her death which was sent round to all the convents. It had been sent to her own mother House but she clearly hadn't been paying attention when it was read out. There would be a copy of it in the library and time to read it before she had to go in to supper. She put the book on the shelf next to her Bible and Missal and went swiftly along the corridor and down the stairs.

The wing containing the guest parlour and chapel with the library and storerooms above was deserted, only the Perpetual Lamp dissipating the twilight. She switched on the overhead light on the narrow stairs and went briskly up them.

The death notices were in a series of books, one for each decade since the founding of the Order. Five large closely written volumes detailing the blameless ends of the various Daughters of Compassion who had died in the several Houses. They were in chronological order which made her task easy. Within a few minutes she was reading with close attention.

''The death is announced of Sister Sophia, born Sophia Brentwood, 5th April, 1963 in Reading. Sister Sophia was an only child, orphaned at the age of nine and reared by an aunt, Miss Mary Brentwood, died 1982. Sister Sophia was educated at the Convent of the Sacred Heart in her home town where she was described as a popular and hard-working pupil, with a definite leaning towards the religious life from an early age. In 1980 she took a two-year course in Primary Schooling at Reading Technical Training College and gained a Diploma with Honours. She taught in the Infants' Section of the Sacred Heart Convent from September 1982 until July 1984 and in September of that year entered the Order as a novice. During her novitiate she impressed her superiors by her dedication, her energy and her devotion to duty. In September 1986 she took her temporary vows and thereafter combined her religious duties with teaching in the Moor School. In September 1987 she took her final vows and was fully professed in the presence of His Lordship the Bishop and the rest of the Community. On the 6th December of that year, having volunteered to test the fire-escape apparatus at Cornwall House, she slipped and fell, the underarm strap tightening around her neck. Both the Prioress, Reverend Mother Ann, and Sister Felicity, Lay Sister, were witnesses of this tragic accident. Despite their attempts and those of Sister Perpetua, Infirmarian, to revive her and the ministrations of the local doctor who was immediately summoned Sister Sophia was pronounced dead. Father Malone in his eulogy after the funeral stressed that though Sister Sophia had died without the consolation of Last Rites her character was such that he believed her already at peace. Her cheerfulness and good humour coupled with a deeply serious attitude to spiritual matters rendered her beloved by her sisters in Christ and by the children she taught, many of whom sent floral tributes. Sister Sophia was in the twenty-sixth year of her age and the third month of her profession.''

On the other side of the page was the standard photograph taken at the time of her final profession. From beneath a wreath of white roses the square, glowing young face smiled out. A plain, healthy, sensible girl who was clearly delighted to consecrate her life to God, Sister Joan thought, and wondered what could have possibly happened to drive her to suicide—if it had been suicide, and for that she had only Sister Perpetua's word. Sister Joan replaced the book and looked further along the shelves for the Register of Novices. Under the rules of the Order a full account of each intending Daughter of Compassion had to be kept on view in the convent where she was training so that other sisters could con-

sult it. On her making her full profession the file was
then placed in the archives, her previous life being considered irrelevant.

She was rather afraid that the item relating to Sister
Magdalen might have been removed already but it was
still there, a neatly typed sheet of paper slipped into a
cellophane folder and clipped inside the larger file.

"Brenda Williams entered the Order as a novice on
2nd September, 1987. She has taken the name of Magdalen. Born and bred in Matlock, Derbyshire, eldest of
three children. Born on 8th June, 1968. Sister Magdalen
is a lively, yet deeply serious girl, somewhat idealistic.
She has a fervent devotion to Our Blessed Lady. She
has been helping out during the recent epidemic of influenza and has made herself very well liked by the
infirmary nuns."

At the bottom someone had typed tersely,

"Sister Magdalen left the Order on the 6th of March,
1988."

Three months after Sister Sophia had died. Was it
possible that the girl had known the death was actually
a suicide and, disillusioned at the official cover-up, decided to leave? It seemed unlikely. She would have to
remember to ask Sister Perpetua if she had mentioned
the matter.

A footfall in the corridor alerted her. She slid the
cellophane folder back into the file and put it on the
shelf, rising as Sister Lucy came in.

"I saw the light on the staircase," the other said by
way of explanation. "Did you enjoy your sandwich,
Sister?"

"She knows I haven't been anywhere near the
kitchen," Sister Joan thought, irritated.

"I decided that if I gave in to my stomach it would
go on dominating me," she answered calmly. "That's
something else I shall have to remember for general

confession. First lack of care for the dumb beast and now disobedience in matters of diet. It isn't a very auspicious beginning.''

"Oh, I won't tell," Sister Lucy said, as she had said before. "I always come out a few minutes ahead of the others to light the candles for Benediction and get the incense burning properly. The charcoal can be tricky. The religious instruction today was very interesting, didn't you think so?''

"Unusual certainly," Sister Joan said cautiously.

"It was a pity you had to leave so soon. Reverend Mother Ann explained everything so beautifully. We cannot neglect the female aspect of God.''

"But Our Blessed Lady was not a goddess," Sister Joan said, forgetting caution. "She was a human being, Sister, and the fact that many of the titles given to her were originally bestowed upon Astarte and Isis doesn't alter the fact.''

"She was in the line of succession, like her mother Saint Anne," Sister Lucy said. Her voice had the patient note of one explaining something to a rather backward child. "Now that we are in the Aquarian age it is time for the Messiah to come again. Who will be privileged to bear Him a second time? Eh, Sister Joan?''

She gave a curious little skip, half mischief, half expectation, and went away, padding softly over the carpet into the corridor.

"But He will return as a king in glory," Sister Joan said in bewilderment, staring after her. "He won't be born all over again.''

The cloistered silence of the library pressed her round. She waited a few moments and then went down quietly into the now candlelit chapel. The others sisters were filing in and the put-put-putting of an ancient car outside announced the arrival of Father Malone. Did Father Malone know that Reverend Mother Ann was filling the heads of her nuns with a heady mixture of gnostic heresy and exaggerated mariolatry? She rather doubted it, having summed up the little priest as the pure-hearted not over-intelligent product of a rural Seminary. Certainly she could hardly ask him. Loyalty to one's Prioress was important. She would have to weigh it against her greater loyalty to the doctrine of the Faith. Certainly discussion within the Church was freer and more unconventional now. All of this might be no more than intellectual juggling with ideas designed to impress the sisters with the brilliance of their Superior. She would have to wait and see. Meanwhile she bowed her head, beginning the Five Glorious Mysteries in unison with her sisters, feeling as the beads slid through her fingers the usual lessening of tension. It was only half way through the service that she realised that the Benediction had preceded supper which was a reversal of the normal convent routine.

Filing out with the others she took the opportunity to whisper to Sister Katherine,

"Benediction was early tonight?"

"No." Sister Katherine looked blank for a moment, then smiled. "Ah, you came on Saturday, didn't you? You won't know the timetable yet. On Saturdays and Sundays supper is before Benediction but on weekdays it is afterwards when we have had our recreation. Father Malone has quite a large area to cover and this makes things easier for him to get round."

An innocuous reason but in practice it meant that the sisters would have two and a half hours of solid religious instruction and worship with no break to lift their energies, and it also meant that the benediction after which the nuns retired to their cells for the night had been replaced by a late meal which struck her as an untidy way in which to end the day.

The trouble with me, she thought wryly, is that I am

too accustomed to the routine at my mother House. The Prioress has the right to set her own timetable to suit her particular convent.

In the recreation room she took a square of canvas from the table and some lengths of tapestry wool. She would begin on a set of cushion-covers, she decided. The old longing to have a paintbrush in her hand still surfaced now and then, but could generally be sublimated into other work.

The Prioress was not there which was something of a relief. Those amused dark eyes above the high cheekbones and the sweetly smiling mouth made her uneasy.

"How did you get on at the school this morning, Sister?"

The delicate-looking Sister Martha had taken a seat next to her. This was the nun in charge of the garden, she remembered, and thought again how unsuited the other seemed to heavy manual work.

"It was exhausting but enjoyable," she answered. "It's five years since I stood in front of a class and I was quite nervous that I'd mess it up, but it went off without anything dreadful happening. I'm even hoping a few of the pupils will return tomorrow morning."

Sister Martha laughed.

"I could never teach in a school," she confided. "I was one of eight children and when I entered the religious life the only thing I could think was 'Thank heavens, I won't have to toilet-train any more little sisters and brothers.'"

"Plants are more docile," Sister Joan said.

"Don't believe it." Sister Martha laughed again. "Some plants are exceedingly difficult to get along with. Have you ever tried to make friends with a very thorny rose bush or tried to persuade an ivy bush not to reach out and cling to the nearest wall?"

"Don't you have help in the garden?" Sister Joan said. "The grounds here are very large."

"Well, each sister is supposed to lend a hand when she can spare time from her other duties, but too often that makes for a real muddle. Sister Sophia drew up a work plan that was very practical but we didn't stick to it unfortunately."

"That was a sad accident." Sister Joan glanced at her companion but the other said only,

"Very sad. In my opinion the apparatus ought to have been tested during the day with all the sisters present. However my opinion was not sought."

"Did you know Sister Magdalen?" She risked asking the question since the other nuns were still drifting into the room and for a moment she and Sister Martha were side by side with nobody next to them in the semicircle of chairs.

"I saw her occasionally. Why?"

"It always interests me when a novice decides to leave. I recall my own doubts and fears."

"Do you? I never had any," Sister Martha said, looking faintly surprised. "No, I saw her once or twice, that's all. She always looked very happy."

Outward appearances seldom told the full story but as far as Sister Joan could make out the novice had genuinely enjoyed her life, had given nobody the slightest reason to suspect that she was planning to leave.

"I brought you a piece of pie." Sister Perpetua came up, holding the triangular wedge wrapped in a paper napkin. "Sister Lucy mentioned that you never went to get anything from Sister Margaret."

So much for not telling. Thanking her, Sister Joan took the pie and bit into it with relish. It was apple pie, faintly flavoured with cinnamon, and tasting even more delicious because she was starving.

"Sister Joan was saying that she was interested in the reasons for novices deciding to leave the religious life," Sister Martha said. "We were speaking of Sister Magdalen."

"Oh, that was a great surprise," Sister Perpetua said promptly, sitting down. "She was always smiling. I was very surprised when she left."

"Did she say goodbye?"

"Why, no. Those who leave the Order never do."

"I only thought—she was helping out during the influenza epidemic, not as isolated as novices usually are."

"Those were exceptional circumstances," Sister Martha said primly. "When the illness had run its course the novices naturally returned to the Novitiate."

Clearly there was nothing to be gained by more questioning. The only ones who might know something were the three novices with whom Sister Magdalen had been in training, and there was no way of contacting them with Mother Emmanuel standing guard. It would be necessary to tell the pugnacious Johnny Russell that she had failed dismally. She finished off the slice of apple pie, wishing it were more, and reminding herself that now she must add greed to her general confession.

A word amid the conversations going on broke through her distraction. She raised her head sharply. Solstice. That word again, spoken casually by Sister Katherine who was embroidering smocking on what looked like a baby's dress.

"What did you say, Sister?"

Sister Katherine was young, in her mid-twenties, with an anonymous face. She answered at once in her calm low voice that matched the placid eyes.

"I was just saying, Sister, that when I've finished this I must start on the Solstice costumes."

"Solstice is a pagan festival surely?"

"To mark the longest day in the year," Sister Katherine nodded. "Oh, we don't keep it as they did in the old days. Of course not. The local farmers keep up the tradition of having a picnic on that day and choosing a solstice queen. We hold a bazaar and help out with the costumes. The Catholic population in this area is small and scattered. This gives them a chance to get together and some of the Protestants join in, which is good for ecumenical relations."

Sister Joan wanted to argue that Christmas and Easter were surely the obvious festivals on which people could get together, but the Church had always made use of the pagan feasts, building the new upon the old, turning local gods into obscure saints. There was nothing here to worry her save the feeling that, in her passion for the past, this Prioress was not merely looking back with nostalgia but actually regressing.

"Evil is an absolute only in heaven," her own Novice Mistress had said. "Those people who sacrificed their children to Moloch were not evil. They were worshipping in the manner they believed would please their gods. The world has evolved since then. For us to turn back the clock would be evil because we would be closing our eyes to the deeper wisdom we have attained over the centuries. Evil is a turning back on the road to perfection."

"I'm sorry to come so late to Recreation."

Reverend Mother Ann had glided in, bringing with her the elegance and charm that made Sister Joan feel uncomfortable as if her Superior were playing the role of a model nun in some play or other.

"We were talking about Solstice," Sister Perpetua said, adding defiantly, "Not that I agree it should still be encouraged."

"Sister Perpetua is the Puritan among us," Reverend Mother Ann said lightly. "She will be reminding us next that holly and mistletoe derive from the ancient Druid faith and were merely grafted on to Christmas. I was called away to the telephone.''

"Not bad news, Reverend Mother?" Sister Martha looked anxious.

"No, no." The Prioress seated herself, the folds of her purple habit falling gracefully from her narrow waist. "It was from Sister Magdalen—Brenda Williams, I ought to say."

"She telephoned you?" Sister Joan couldn't repress the startled question.

"Sister Felicity actually answered the phone. We were going over the supplies of aspirin and indigestion tablets she needs when she stocks up on her first-aid cupboard. How nuns can possibly suffer from indigestion! Where was I? Oh, yes. The child rang me up from some commune somewhere or other. She wanted me to inform her parents that she has joined some cult or other, one of those free-love places where children and everything else are held in common. Quite shocking, but also unfortunately attractive to young people."

"Where is this commune?"

Sister Joan was glad that Sister Perpetua had asked the question.

"She wouldn't be specific," Reverend Mother Ann said. "Somewhere in Wales, I believe. I felt very strongly that she ought to telephone them herself but she refused. She is probably afraid that they will persuade her to go home."

"Are you going to telephone them?" Sister Perpetua asked.

"To set their minds at rest," the other said. "Of course they have been imagining her still in the Novitiate and I was under the impression that she had returned home to Derbyshire. Our responsibility for her ended when Sister Felicity drove her to the station. The problem is that I still feel responsible though there's no reason for it.''

"You are too kind-hearted, Reverend Mother Ann,'' Sister Dorothy put in.

"Is that a fault? I plead guilty then.'' The Prioress laughed softly, hand to her mouth.

"I read once that when any virtue is carried to excess it becomes a vice,'' Sister Lucy said.

"And what's your virtue run to vice?'' Sister David asked her teasingly.

"Arranging flowers,'' Sister Lucy said promptly. "I am apt to spend hours and hours on the flowers in the chapel until sometimes I forget to come to supper.''

"I spend too much time writing up my spiritual diary,'' Sister David said. "I am always trying to express what I mean to say in the most perfect language possible, forgetting that it isn't meant to be a masterpiece.''

The talk, light and inconsequential, went on. Sister Joan, a vague pattern forming on the piece of canvas, thought of spiritual diaries. Every nun kept a private record of her spiritual struggles and progress or lack of it. When she died the diary was kept in the convent files for one never knew when evidence might be required in the event of a possible enquiry into the cause for canonisation of someone or other. She suspected that some diaries were written with an eye towards that possibility. Sister Sophia would have written such a diary. It would be in the private files, accessible only to the Prioress and to any Church officials who might later request it.

"What of you, Sister Joan?'' Reverend Mother Ann spoke gaily. "What is your besetting virtue?''

"Too much enjoyment of good food,'' Sister Joan said, neatly sidestepping what she sensed was a challenge.

"One would never guess it from your figure."

"That's because none of my virtues is excessive," she parried.

"I don't follow this at all. It's far too clever for me," Sister Martha said humbly. The dark, smiling eyes flicked towards her.

"Of course not, dear," the Prioress said with viperish gentleness. "Sister Perpetua, you have not told us your virtue yet."

"Truth," said Sister Perpetua. Her reddish brows were knitted and the crumples in her white skin sharp as pleats of linen. "I am never satisfied with less, Reverend Mother." Now why didn't I have the courage to say that instead of evading the issue with clever talk? Sister Joan felt a pang of shame.

"What is truth? said jesting Pilate," the Prioress said, rising. "Come, it is supper time which will give Sister Joan a chance to indulge her virtue to excess."

NINE

✠ ✠ ✠

It was too much to hope that Johnny Russell would decide not to come. Throughout the next morning while she taught the children, all of whom had returned, she wrestled with the problem of how to tell him. By the time twelve thirty came and her pupils had departed she was almost craven enough to mount up and ride back to the convent without waiting. She would not have got very far. The two Romany children had scarcely disappeared on the pony they jointly rode before he came striding towards her.

"Come into the schoolroom." She led the way, feeling his impatience like a swelling wind. "Did you find good lodgings?"

"Good enough. Did you find out anything, Sister?"

"Entirely by chance. Sister Magdalen, Brenda that is, telephoned the Mother Prioress while we were at recreation last evening."

"Did she say where she was?" His face had flushed with eagerness.

"Apparently on a commune somewhere in Wales. It sounded like one of those peace and pot experiments left over from the sixties. She asked Reverend Mother

Ann to tell her parents, which she will do this morning.''

"On a commune in Wales?" he echoed. "That doesn't make sense."

"Why not?" Sister Joan sat opposite the young man on one of the small desks.

"If she left the convent she'd have gone home; she'd have come back to me. She wouldn't run off to Wales to live on a commune. That's the craziest story I ever heard."

"Johnny, try to understand what it's like to be a novice," she urged gently. "For six months she had lived in one small house. The Novitiate is separate from the convent proper. Apparently she helped out when there was an epidemic of influenza shortly after her arrival but after that she went back into seclusion. A two-year period of tough mental and physical and spiritual testing. She seemed happy enough according to everyone I've spoken to, but obviously she decided she'd made a mistake and she left. Sister Felicity, one of the lay sisters, drove her to the station. Now it's the wrong way to look at it but some girls if they leave the Novitiate feel a sense of failure. They ought to feel proud that they had had the clear sight to realise the life wasn't right for them and the courage to turn back, but some don't see it like that. She may have met up with some members of the commune on the train and decided to go with them, to think over her next step."

"Bullshit," Johnny said flatly. "Sorry, Sister, but that's what you're giving me. I knew I couldn't rely on a nun to tell me straight."

"I am telling you straight." She bit back a sharp reply telling herself that he was too worried to remember his manners. "Why is it—why isn't it possible that that's exactly what happened?"

"Because Brenda would have rung her mum and dad

herself even if she had gone off to a commune. She had a good relationship with them and they'd have been quite pleased to hear she'd changed her mind about being a nun. I told you they always liked me. Who took this telephone call? You?''

"I was at recreation. The Prioress came in and told us that Sister Felicity had actually answered the phone and then handed it to her. Johnny, you're not suggesting that two professed nuns, one of them the Superior of the convent, concocted some tale that wasn't true, are you?''

"Do you reckon this Sister—Perpet?''

"Perpetua.''

"Do you reckon she was telling you the truth?''

"She seemed to be.''

But as she spoke Sister Joan hesitated, remembering the nervous grimaces, the hand clutching the crucifix. There were nuns who became hysterical, imagining all manner of strange happenings in their convents. She judged Sister Perpetua to be in her early fifties, perhaps experiencing a late and difficult menopause.

"She seemed to be,'' she repeated. "I'm the new girl here. I don't know anyone well enough yet to make a reasoned evaluation. But there is something else. One of the old sisters in the infirmary was anxious about something. Whatever it was she obviously didn't want to tell the Prioress here.''

"Have you asked her about it?''

"Mother Frances died.'' Seeing the expression on his face she added hastily, "She was over ninety.''

"Can't you ask the Prioress?'' he suggested.

" 'Excuse me, Reverend Mother, have you and Sister Felicity covered up a suicide to look like an accident and lied about a novice who left here three months ago?' No, I couldn't ask the Prioress, Johnny. She is my Superior and I don't have the right to gossip about what are merely suspicions with anybody.''

"Shouldn't be talking to me then, should you?" he said.

"You haven't given me much choice, have you?" she said wryly. "Look, I can understand how you feel."

"How can you? You're a nun," Johnny said.

"I wasn't born in this habit, you know," Sister Joan said, amused. "I was thirty years old before I entered the religious life. I stuck it out and I enjoy it, but that doesn't automatically set me apart from the rest of the human race, you know."

"I think it does," Johnny said, adding, "Not in a nasty way perhaps."

"For small relief much thanks. I need more time if I'm to find out anything. I can't spend all my time asking questions about two people I never even knew. I have my religious duties as well as my teaching. Can you stay on in the district for a few more days?"

"I took a fortnight off," he said, "but I can't hang round doing nothing."

"Are you still friendly with Mr. and Mrs. Williams?" He nodded.

"Why not ring them up?" she suggested. "They're bound to let you know if the Prioress phoned up about Sister Magdalen—Brenda, that is."

"What are you going to do?" he asked.

"Poke around," she said firmly. "There are records kept on all the novices and nuns. I have only seen the ones that everybody can see so far. If I bend the rules a little I can take a look at the others."

"Might you not get into trouble?" For the first time he looked slightly doubtful.

"I might." She couldn't repress a smile at the look on his face. "However, one thing I've learned that be-

ing a nun hasn't altered is that people who aren't willing
to risk getting into trouble usually don't get things done.
Oh, and be discreet when you talk to the Williamses.''

"I'm phoning from the Lake District," he said
promptly.

"I don't want you telling deliberate lies," she said
hastily.

"I won't," he promised. "I'll just bend the truth a
bit. Is there anything else I can do?"

"If there's a newspaper office in town you might get
hold of a copy of the inquest on Sister Sophia. She died
in December."

"I'll do that." He looked more cheerful at the prospect of having definite action to take.

"I'll see you tomorrow and let you know if there's
anything to report," she said.

"If it wasn't so worrying," he said, standing up,
"I'd quite enjoy this, you know. It's a bit like Sherlock
Holmes and Doctor Watson, isn't it?"

"Not really," she said dryly. "I've never taken co-
caine and I can't play the violin." It was slightly dis-
concerting to emerge from the school building and find
Grant Tarquin stroking Lilith, his smile becoming a
questioning one as his eyes rested on Johnny.

"Mr. Tarquin, good morning." She winced inwardly
at the heartiness of her tone. "This is Mr. Russell who
is hiking in the district."

"I thought he looked rather large to be one of your
pupils, Sister." Grant Tarquin shook hands with Johnny
amiably. "Are you planning to stay around for a while
or move on south?"

"I thought I'd stay on, take some walks on the
moor," Johnny said.

"In that case get yourself a good Ordnance Survey
map if you haven't already," Grant Tarquin advised.
"The moor can be treacherous, bogs in places and the

mist rolling in when you least expect it. Done much walking?''

"Some. It's a hobby of mine.''

"The convent where our little Community lives was once the Tarquin family home,'' Sister Joan said, "but it's not open to tourists I'm afraid. Bodmin itself is a very ancient town.''

"I must catch up with my sightseeing. Thanks for your help, Sister.''

Johnny shouldered his backpack and strode off.

"You really ought to be more careful, Sister,'' Grant Tarquin said, looking after him.

"I beg your pardon?'' Sister Joan looked at him.

"The times are pretty violent now, even in rural districts,'' he said. "This school is in an isolated spot too.''

"Mr. Tarquin, I really don't think you have any cause for concern,'' Sister Joan said, sternly repressing a grin. "He was a perfectly respectable young man who happens to be on a holiday and wanted directions. I was never in the slightest danger.''

"Unfortunately your habit may not always protect you,'' he warned. "You must excuse my interest. The truth is that I feel a kind of inherited responsibility for the sisters now living in the old family home. I keep a weather eye open for them whenever I can.''

"Oh dear.'' The grin escaped, dimpling her cheek. "That makes me feel as if I were on probation or something.''

"Not in the least, Sister.'' His smile matched hers. "I am simply always happier when all the sisters are tucked up at Cornwall House. It's a family failing if you wish to call it a failing.''

"Oh?'' She glanced at him curiously, seeing that the smile had faded and his dark eyes were sombre.

"My wife was killed ten years ago,'' he said abruptly.

"She was driving the car I'd given her for our second wedding anniversary. We weren't living here then but in Taunton. Anyway she swerved to avoid a Sister of Mercy who was crossing the road and crashed into a wall. She died instantly and the child she was expecting with her."

"That was a terrible thing to happen."

"Thank you for not saying it was God's Will," he said wryly. "Anyway I felt, probably illogically, that by avoiding that nun she had saved a valuable life. I've felt ever since that the life of a religious is somehow precious. Does that sound stupid?"

"I would say that all life is precious," she answered cautiously, "but I'm sure that the sisters appreciate your concern."

"Unhappily I'm not always around," he said. "That poor girl who fell when they were having the fire drill— if I'd known what they were going to do I'd have offered to test it myself or send someone over. It was a fool-hardy risk to take and it ended in tragedy."

"Did you know Sister Sophia?"

"Yes, of course. She taught here," he reminded her. "Very nice person, lively and good-hearted, very good with the children. Her death was a shame, a great shame."

"Yes indeed." She spoke vaguely, hoisting herself to Lilith's broad back.

Grant Tarquin believed, like everybody else, that the death had been an accident. She wondered how far his somewhat idealistic view of nuns would change if he were told that three of them had covered up a suicide to look like an accident.

"I won't keep you, Sister." He stood back. "In future just be a little more careful about giving directions to stray young men."

The warning irritated her. There was patronage in it,

the faint playfulness with which some people were apt to address nuns, as if people who chose to live in convents were half-witted. She bit back the sharp retort that hovered on her lips and said amiably, "I'll take good care. 'Bye."

She was late for lunch again, she realised, though it had been made clear to her that such tardiness would not be accounted a fault since she had to tidy away and lock up before riding back. Still she had better have some explanation ready if anyone else found out she was regularly seeing a young hiker. The prospect of having her reputation called in question brought a smile of pure mischief into her eyes. The mischief faded as she reconsidered the long talk she had had with both her visitors. Johnny Russell was in love with Brenda Williams and highly suspicious of the way she had left so suddenly and not returned home.

Sister Joan, being somewhat more mature than the pugnacious Mr. Russell, had learned that people didn't always act in character, but Brenda's abrupt departure had been the prelude to her disappearance—unless she really was on a commune in Wales.

"Have you eaten, Sister?" The plump lay sister lay in waiting for her, bouncing out of the back door like a jack in the box. "Reverend Mother Ann said I was to be sure to see that you got something. I forgot the coffee this morning for you."

"I was so busy that I didn't have time to eat or drink anything," Sister Joan said.

"Children can be tiring," Sister Margaret said. "My mother always used to say that when the Good Lord sent the blessings of children He also sent each blessing wrapped up in a bundle of troubles. She knew what she was talking about too, poor woman, having borne nine with myself as the fifth. Come into the kitchen now and eat."

Sister Joan hadn't yet entered the kitchen which proved to be a cavernous place that looked as if it had been intended as a basement but had crept up to ground-floor level when nobody was looking. The walls were a light bilious green with rag matting covering the stone floor and the tiles cracked round the double sink and huge old-fashioned oven.

"More homely than the rest of the house, isn't it?" Sister Margaret said happily.

"A lot," Sister Joan said feelingly.

"Holy poverty," Sister Margaret said, her round face beaming, "is much easier to hold to in a place like this than in a parlour."

It was a delicately expressed criticism of the Prioress.

"This looks delicious," Sister Joan said sitting down at one end of the long scrubbed wooden table.

"My vegetable omelette is fit for a bishop," Sister Margaret said proudly. "Poor Sister Sophia was very fond of it, God rest her soul."

"It must have been a terrible shock to everybody when she died," Sister Joan said, spooning up the thick blend of vegetables and spices.

"Not long before Christmas either," Sister Margaret said sadly, pouring two cups of coffee and taking a seat at the corner of the table. With her veil pushed back and her sleeves rolled up over her muscular arms she looked as if she were auditioning for the role of the Nurse in *Romeo and Juliet*, though she lacked the salt-iness of the latter's vocabulary.

"You were not there?" Sister Joan dunked her brown bread with blissful disregard for the conventions.

"I was in bed," Sister Margaret said. "Sister Felicity and I sleep there. In the old larder and the old pantry. They make very suitable cells. And we are near to the infirmary so if one of the older sisters requires anything during the night or is taken ill we can fetch Sister

Perpetua. Sister Felicity had gone to the chapel to complete her Advent meditation.''

"At eleven at night?'' Sister Joan raised an eyebrow.

"Sister Felicity has arduous duties,'' Sister Margaret said a trifle defensively. "It is often near midnight before she can get away to fulfil her religious duties.''

"And she was doing that on the night Sister Sophia—?''

"She and Reverend Mother Ann,'' Sister Margaret nodded. "Then they decided to test the fire-escape apparatus. Sister Sophia was doing penance in the chapel and offered to be the guinea-pig as she was younger and more agile—it was a great tragedy.''

"I believe that Sister Sophia was very popular,'' Sister Joan said.

"Oh, a very good girl,'' Sister Margaret said promptly. "She did wonders with the children, I believe. My own view is that she had a black-out.''

"I thought the strap slipped.''

"Yes, it did, but it seems odd she didn't make a last-minute grab at it to prevent its looping round her neck. Of course she was holding on with both hands to the window-ledge to test the strength of the main straps but one would have thought it would have been instinctive. That's what makes me think she could have had a momentary black-out.''

"Was she subject to them?''

"She hadn't been looking well,'' Sister Margaret said. "She was always very jolly, you see, lovely sense of humour and yet very serious about spiritual matters. You know how it is.''

Sister Joan nodded. A sense of humour often betokened a deeply spiritual nature.

"Didn't Saint Teresa say, 'Lord defend me from sullen saints?' '' she said.

"Indeed she did and quite correct too,'' Sister Mar-

garet said. "Well, Sister Sophia was the kind of nun
Saint Teresa would have approved. But a few weeks
before she died—two or three weeks it was—she came
into the kitchen after school one day, the way you're
here now. I think I'd made an omelette that day too.
Yes, it was an omelette because she was pushing a bit
of it round and round on her plate. She had a funny
look on her face."

"What sort of funny?"

"Funny peculiar, not funny comical," Sister Margaret said. "Like her mind had gone blank. I said
something to her and she jumped and looked at me and
then she gave a laugh—not a real sort of laugh. Strained
more like."

"And?"

"She excused herself and went out," Sister Margaret
said. "I wondered at the time if she suffered from *petit
mal*. One of my sisters did—my blood sisters I mean.
In the middle of a sentence she'd stop dead for a few
seconds and a blank look would come over her face and
then she'd carry on again as if her brain had missed a
few beats."

"Did she do that often? Sister Sophia I mean?"

The other shook her head.

"Only the one time as far as I saw. But after that she
went round looking worried. No, not exactly worried,
more pressured. I thought she was perhaps working too
hard or doing too much penance."

Sister Joan reflected. The Order of the Daughters of
Compassion advocated moderate penance, but over-
enthusiastic sisters who carried penance to the threshold of masochistic delight were sternly cautioned. From
all she had heard Sister Sophia had not seemed that type
at all.

"Did you mention this to anyone?" she asked at last.

"No." Sister Margaret shook her head. "I didn't

think of it until later. And of course I wasn't called to the inquest. It's only lately that I've thought—Mother Frances said something about the matter. Before her death, I mean.''

''About Sister Sophia being ill?''

''No, not that. She was very old, you know, apt to repeat herself occasionally but she was quite logical in her head. Wonderful for her age. On the other hand she now and then came out with something that weird that made you realise how old she was.''

There was no point in hurrying the other. Obviously Sister Margaret relished what she would have called a nice chat.

''A couple of days before she died,'' the nun was continuing. ''Before Mother Frances died, I mean. She had gone very frail. Very old but still quite sharp mentally, apart from one or two things she said that didn't make much sense. I'd taken her a nice bowl of soup and she asked me why Sister Sophia hadn't been to see her recently. Then she caught herself up before I could say anything and said, 'I forgot. The poor girl died, didn't she? Fell out of the window. If you ask me she found out there's a gospel too many.' ''

''A gospel too many?'' Sister Joan repeated the phrase. ''What did she mean?''

''That's exactly what I said,'' Sister Margaret said. 'Whatever do you mean, Mother Frances?' I said. She shook her head and told me the soup smelt good.''

''There are four gospels,'' Sister Joan said thoughtfully. ''Matthew, Mark, Luke, John.''

''Well everybody knows that, Sister,'' the other said. ''Maybe she was going a bit senile?''

''Oh no,'' Sister Margaret said promptly. ''She was apt to repeat herself now and then but she always made perfect sense.''

"Did Sister Magdalen talk a lot with Mother Frances?" Sister Joan asked abruptly.

"Sister Magdalen?" Sister Margaret looked slightly puzzled at the change of subject. "No, I don't think so. The novices came to help when the influenza epidemic was on. Why?"

"I was wondering why she left so suddenly."

"Oh, one can never tell with young girls," Sister Margaret said. "You think she might have been upset by the accident? She stayed on for three months if she was and Sister Hilaria said she seemed radiant. We really believed she had a strong vocation."

Somewhere in the infirmary a bell tinkled.

"That'll be Sister Andrew," Sister Margaret said with obvious reluctance as she rose. "She can be difficult. A wonderful woman." She sighed slightly as she spoke.

"And I must get on with preparing some lessons for tomorrow," Sister Joan said, also rising. "Oh, by the way, what did you say to Sister Sophia when she was looking so blank? You said she gave a strained sort of laugh."

"Well, it wasn't very important," Sister Margaret said, thinking. "It was a little joke as far as I remember. I said something like—if the Archangel Gabriel came and blew his trumpet in your ear you wouldn't hear him. Just a silly joke. Nothing more."

TEN

✠ ✠ ✠

Sister Joan was not preparing lessons. Seated cross legged on the floor with her habit bunched under her seat in the time-honoured practice of nuns she was writing out what in her own mind she thought of, somewhat self-consciously, as her detection notes. She laid down her pen now and turned back the pages of her pad to recapitulate.

Events: Brenda Williams entered the Novitiate on 2nd September, 1987.

Sister Sophia entered the Novitiate in September, 1984. Was fully professed in September, 1987 (same month Brenda entered Novitiate).

Sister Magdalen (Brenda) left the convent on 16th February, 1988.

People: Reverend Mother Ann, daughter of noted archaeologist, aged approx. 45. Professed 15 years ago and is now serving second term of office as Prioress. Very advanced theological notions. Wears nail polish and perfume.

Mother Emmanuel, mid-fifties, helps out with novices. Adores Prioress.

Sister Hilaria, Novice Mistress. Mystic or hysteric? Probably inefficient.

Sister Dorothy, Librarian. Intelligent white rabbit. Officious.

Sister Lucy, Sacristan. Tale-bearer and too sweet to be true.

Sister David, another white rabbit but shyer.

Sister Perpetua, Infirmarian, worried about situation here. Either lied at the inquest about circumstances surrounding Sister Sophia's death or is lying to me about the whole thing. But why should she?

Sisters Martha, and Katherine. Nice but not intellectual.

Sisters Mary Concepta, Andrew and Gabrielle, elderly. Mother Frances evidently didn't confide in them.

Sister Felicity, Lay Sister, efficient, was with Prioress in chapel on night of Sister Sophia's death.

Sister Margaret, likes chatting. May be subconsciously worried hence her gossiping to me.

Observations: Rules here not exactly lax but not strictly enforced. Prioress likes her comfort and may have her favourites i.e. Sister Felicity, Mother Emmanuel, Sister Lucy?

Grant Tarquin seems to take a proprietory interest in convent and school. Sublimation of feelings for dead wife?

Much interest and emphasis on pagan goddess cults and their links with Our Lady.

Questions: Why did Sister Sophia give a strained laugh when Sister Margaret made a little joke about the Archangel Gabriel?

Why did Sister Sophia, immediately after her profession, lose her gaiety and become morose?

Did Sister Sophia hang herself or was it an accident?

If it was an accident why test the apparatus so late at night? Why did Sister Perpetua tell me it was suicide?

If it was suicide why did Sister Sophia kill herself?

Why did Brenda leave the convent so abruptly? If she

was upset about Sister Sophia's death she would surely
have left at the time, not waited until the middle of
February. If she was unhappy in the Novitiate why did
nobody appear to notice the fact?

Why didn't she inform her parents that she had left?

Is she really on a commune in Wales? If not then
why would the Prioress take the trouble of lying to us?
She doesn't know I have any interest in the girl.

What did Mother Frances mean when she talked
about an extra gospel?

Having reached the end she heaved a sigh. As a de-
tective, she decided ruefully, she made an excellent nun.
And that wasn't true either. No deeply religious nun
would have marked all the faults and failings of her
sisters, let alone set them down on paper. Feeling thoroughly ashamed of herself Sister Joan tore the thin
sheets into tiny pieces and went along the corridor to
flush them down the toilet. She would concentrate on
her proper work and leave doubts and suspicions in that
region of her mind where she had locked up all forbidden things.

To her relief the religious instruction period that preceded the Benediction was conducted by Sister Dorothy
who stuck firmly to the Confessions of Saint Augustine
and their relevance in the life of a modern religious.

At recreation the talk centered on the good and bad
points of the local dentist who was regarded as a patron
saint by Sister Martha and as first cousin to Torquemada
by everybody else. It was all rather dull and very reassuring.

In bed that night for the first time in years Sister Joan
dreamed of Jacob. He was driving a car and she sat
beside him, stealing glances at his craggy profile, wondering how the genes of a third-generation refugee from
somewhere beyond the Pale could have united with the
genes of a Whitechapel tailor to produce that blending

of flesh and bone that was unique, hers to savour in all
its rough masculine beauty. Then she realised with a
little shock that she was stark naked, and that the man
driving the car was Grant Tarquin. She reached for the
door-handle, having some idea in her mind of jumping
out as the vehicle slowed to go round a corner, but as
she turned her head Reverend Mother Ann suddenly
leaned from the back seat and pinioned her with a lavender scented claw.

She sat bolt upright, sweat pearling her face. So much
for custody of the mind. In sleep it went roving down
Freudian byways.

Her cell seemed airless. Still sitting up she allowed
the moonlit shapes within the room to resolve themselves into the few items of furniture. Shelf with its
books, plastic curtain behind which her other garments
bulged slightly, basin and ewer—her mouth was dry and
with that realisation came the remembrance that she
had completely forgotten to fill the ewer with cold water
ready for the morning ablutions. The way things were
going, she thought resignedly, by the time general confession came on Friday everybody else might as well
sit down because her list of faults was getting longer
every day.

Certainly she couldn't go until morning with her
tongue clinging to the roof of her mouth. The bathrooms, two of them, and their adjoining toilets were at
the end of the passage. An overhead light burned dimly
red when she opened the door.

House shoes and cloak took only a couple of seconds
to don. She bent to pick up the ewer and went out into
the corridor. Further along a door opened and closed
swiftly behind the small figure of Sister Lucy who went
on down the passage without looking round. Not to the
bathroom however but to the head of the narrow flight
of stairs that connected with the kitchen. Without

knowing quite why, Sister Joan set down the ewer,
pulled her door to within an inch of being closed and
followed, her rubber soles making no noise on the linoleum. The other was at the foot of the stairs, pausing
to light a lantern. Sister Joan had a brief glimpse of the
little, catlike face illuminated by the brilliance before
Sister Lucy turned the wick lower. As Sister Joan hesitated in the angle of the stairs the bulky figure of Sister
Felicity emerged from her cell off the kitchen. Together
the two figures moved towards the back door.

Wild theories of midnight assignations jostled in her
mind. All nonsense, of course. but convents were usually peaceful places during the grand silence. Certainly
she had never heard of nuns creeping around with lan-
terns in what must be the early hours of the morning.

They were not breaking the grand silence anyway but
gliding noiselessly to the back door. She waited a moment and then descended the narrow stairs. In the
kitchen faint greyish ashes lay in the wide, old-fashioned
hearth with the stone bake oven at its side.

She moved to the back door and bit her lip with annoyance as it failed to yield to her hand. It must have
been locked again on the outside. Now she could choose
either to return meekly to her cell or to leave the house
by another exit.

She chose the latter course, stepping out into the passage that ran past the infirmary, hearing the muffled
music of three old ladies gently snoring in concert as
she went by the door. In the main hall another light
burned dimly, barely revealing the carved wainscoting,
the half-open door beyond which lay antechamber and
parlour. Here she hesitated and then, following instinct,
stepped within and stole across to the double doors.
They were not locked and she entered the parlour feeling a mixture of emotions. Some guilt because what
she was doing went against all her natural inclinations

as well as her ethical training, a growing excitement and a sudden longing for the austere purity of the parlour where Reverend Mother Agnes held the reins of authority.

Yet it was a beautiful room, its faded elegance softened by the moonlight that arched through the windows. The long curtains were still held back in graceful folds and the statue was transmuted into deep ivory.

Sister Joan crossed the room to take a closer look. Any casual glance would have identified that slender, cloaked figure with the crown on the small head as the Virgin. Both hands were held, palms outward a little away from the body in what looked like the familiar pose of acceptance and blessing. At the front of the neat little crown a crescent moon trembled. She had been with Jacob when they had stopped to look at the statue of Isis in the Museum. ''The forerunner and prototype of your Virgin Mary,'' he had said provocatively. ''She was married to her brother Osiris, but Osiris was murdered and dismembered by the other brother, Set, and Isis roamed the world in search of the missing pieces. Finally they were all put together again and Isis bore Horus. After which Osiris promptly died all over again and went to rule the Underworld.''

''So?'' She had assumed the expression of a rather backward pupil faced by an intelligent tutor.

''So you tell me the difference between that and the Holy Trinity.''

''I think,'' she had said hesitantly, abandoning the pose, ''that the idea of a Trinity has always been implicit in human consciousness. All those pre-Christian cults were gropings towards the reality.''

Isis or Mary, the wooden statue had a grace, a purity of line that transcended the fashionable parlour.

Sister Joan crossed herself, murmured a brief prayer for guidance and left the parlour. To draw the bolts on

the front door might rouse someone. She turned towards the further wing where the narrow passage led to
the chapel. At least if anyone saw her she could say that
she was doing penance. It was not an excuse that would
have been accepted for one moment by Reverend
Mother Agnes, but here where nuns apparently did penance and held fire drills in the middle of the night it
might be taken as normal.

The chapel door was locked. She had turned the handle
softly but it resisted her effort, and she stood, staring at
the closed and secret panels.

This was ridiculous. In cities and towns the unfortunate increase in crimes of vandalism had made it necessary to lock up churches in between services, but
every convent maintained an ever open chapel where
any sister or visitor could worship or meditate or simply
sit quietly letting the peaceful atmosphere heal the
problems and strains of the everyday world. It was a
violation of her own rights to be locked out.

The side door through which visitors to the public
parlour came had only a small bolt drawn across it. She
drew it back, blessing whoever oiled the locks, and was
outside again. The chapel windows were too high for
her to see in and there was no convenient ladder lying
around. But there were candles burning within. More
light than the illumination provided by the Perpetual
Lamp streamed through the stained glass. She bit her
lip, trying to hit on some brilliant plan of campaign.
Nothing came to mind.

Meanwhile she was still thirsty and the cold dew was
soaking through the thin soles of her slippers. Feeling
increasingly foolish she trailed round the side of the
building, looking up in exasperation at the glowing
rectangles of glass above her head.

It was then that she noticed the tall water butt placed
close to the side wall within reach of the slanting dor-

mer window that admitted light to the sacristy. She had thought on first seeing it that the architect who had stuck a dormer window in the slanting overhang of a seventeenth-century roof ought to have been condemned to sit and look at it for the rest of his life. Now she sent him a grateful word of thanks for his foresight in providing access to the upper storey.

Being small and wiry had had its advantages in the school gymnasium, enabling her to come out ahead in any exercise requiring balance and dexterity. In races she had generally panted up among the also-rans, but work on the parallel bars and the ceiling ropes had allowed her to compete on equal terms. At school however she had worn leotard, not long nightdress and hampering cloak. She took off cloak and slippers, folded them neatly in the shadow of the rain butt and used the string of the cloak to kilt up the nightgown to knee level.

The butt had iron hoops ringing it round. She reached up, her fingers and toes hooking the metal, took a deep breath and squirmed higher until she was sitting astride the rim. When she looked down she could see the dark sparkle of water within. Now with a little luck she could swing herself to the sloping window and from there reach one of the dormer windows above. A narrow ridge, about four inches wide would give her a toe-hold. The possibility that the upper windows might all be screwed shut entered her mind and was thrust aside.

She raised herself cautiously, balancing on the rim, leaning in towards the wall, one hand reaching up to the overhang of the roof. It was of stone as she had guessed, which would not bend obligingly but would, she hoped, bear her weight.

It bore her slightness easily and she squirmed herself sideways, urging her unused muscles to hoist the rest of her to the coping.

She was alongside the dormer window, pinned like a moth to the rough stone. At least she wouldn't slide off and land with a splash in the rain butt, she thought thankfully.

The ridge was only just above her head. She inched upwards, feeling a surge of triumph as her hands fastened on the projecting sill of the end window. The trick now was not to look down but to continue leaning inwards while her fingers grasped the projecting sash and the ridge scraped skin from her toes.

The window slid up easily and she bent over the sill, allowing her pent breath to escape her and then sliding the lower half of her body within, landing with a faint thump on the floor. In her own ears the thump sounded like an earthquake but she was certain it could not have been heard from below. She rose, wincing as the reality of scraped palms, knees and toes stung her, and softly closed the window.

She was in one of the storerooms. The square shapes of packing-boxes stood all around. The possibility that the inner door might be locked delayed her for a second and then she negotiated a passage between the boxes and tried the handle. It opened easily and she went into the passage that led to the narrow staircase leading down into the chapel. No convenient light burned here. Presumably nobody ever wandered about here after dark. From below came the tinkling of the Sanctus bell. A Mass at this hour held in complete silence? It made no sense at all.

She moved forward along the corridor to the greyish square of light that marked the top of the stairs. She couldn't recall if any of the steps creaked, but she would have to risk it.

None of them did and she gained the small landing at the bend in the staircase with no sound save the hammering of her heart in her ears.

Below, grouped about the Lady Altar, the four novices, demure in their pale smocks with the white collars, knelt in silent devotion, prostrating themselves each time Sister Lucy rang the Sanctus bell. Behind the novices the Prioress stood, flanked by Mother Emmanuel and Sister Felicity, all three bowing in unison with the tinkling bell. Bathed in the soft light of the candles the entire scene had an innocent charm, a purity that was completely unlike her more freakish imaginings.

The bell rang a final time and the novices rose, heads bowed and hands folded, to pass before the older sisters, each novice kneeling briefly for blessing, genuflecting to the high altar and filing silently out.

Sister Lucy was moving from candle to candle, extinguishing each flame. The painted features of the Virgin retreated into shadow again. Only the Perpetual Lamp still glowed. One by one the remaining sisters left the chapel. To Sister Joan's relief Sister Lucy, the last to leave, merely closed the outer door. The idea of having to climb out of the upper windows and shin down the sloping roof to the water butt had been less than attractive. She came down the final fight of stairs and sat down in one of the choir stalls. At that moment she was feeling a complete and utter fool. What she had just seen was clearly an exercise in group worship, unusual only because of the hour at which it was being held, but even that could be explained. Discipline of mind over body was a necessary feature of the religious life and though in the Order of the Daughters of Compassion one was not often roused from sleep to spend an hour in prayer in a cold chapel the personal will still had to be subdued.

She slid to her knees, crossing herself, glad of the sting of her scraped knees and palms since it provided an instant penance. Certainly this night's escapade could never be confessed either in general confession or privately to the chubby little Father Malone. She would wait until some stranger priest visited as happened now and then to give the laity a change of confessor.

It would have been pleasant to stay here and doze for a while with her head on her arms. She resisted the temptation and rose, moved into the aisle, genuflected and went to the door, pausing to dip her fingers into the holy water stoup and blessing herself. The cool water on her brow reminded her again that she was thirsty. She would not however quench her thirst until the morning. Another small slice of penance for foolishness.

Outside was starlight, Venus hanging low with the attendant Sirius ringed with cloud. She went back to the water butt, sternly repressed a feeling of pride when she looked up to trace with her eyes the climb she had taken and retrieved her garments.

She pulled down her nightdress, shrouded herself in the cloak and slid her dirty and scratched feet into her slippers. Re-entering through the visitors' door she went softly along the passage to the main hall again.

Here she hesitated, unwilling to run into any of the other sisters, but the others had dispersed. By now the novices, she assumed, would be tucked up in their beds again. Not until she was in her cell again, the door closed, the betraying cloak hung away, did she sit up in bed as violently as she had done on wakening from the dream, her mouth open with astonishment at her own slow wits.

The four novices, kneeling, their hands joined, their hair glossy in the candlelight. Veronica Stirling's hair carefully combed and curled, another novice with curly red hair. The Prioress had stooped to ruffle it playfully as she gave the blessing. Four pretty novices and not a shaven head among them. Suddenly everything was more puzzling than before.

ELEVEN

✠ ✠ ✠

"Whatever have you done to your hands, Sister?" Sister Katherine exclaimed, staring at them as the former reached for a slice of bread.

They were standing up eating breakfast on the following morning.

"What? Oh, nothing much. I scraped them somewhere."

"It looks just like the stigmata," Sister David said from her other side.

"It isn't," Sister Joan said curtly. "I will have to remember to wear gloves when I go riding, that's all. For heaven's sake don't start any silly rumours."

Sister David looked hurt and moved away. She had cause, Sister Joan thought contritely. Not once yet had she invited her over to help in the school and this morning she had snapped her head off.

She said quickly,

"I was wondering if you could possibly take school tomorrow for me, Sister? I have tried to give you a rest but it's so long since I taught that I am finding it exhausting."

"Gladly, Sister," Sister David said, promptly melting. From her forgiving glance it was obvious that she'd

133

put Sister Joan's snappishness down to tiredness. In which she wasn't far wrong since she hadn't slept a wink after her realisation that one of the strictest rules in the Order was being flouted. Wigs perhaps? No, Reverend Mother Ann had ruffled one girl's hair too energetically for that theory to stick.

"You had better get something from Sister Perpetua for those scratches, Sister," Sister Katherine said.

"I'll go along before I go to school," Sister Joan said, putting down her coffee-cup. She caught up with Sister Perpetua as the latter was on her way to the infirmary and made her request.

"Let me see." Sister Perpetua clucked her tongue as the other spread out her palms. "How did you do that?"

"I've decided to wear gloves for riding in future," Sister Joan evaded.

"I should think so! Come into the dispensary and I'll get you some salve. I pound it up myself from a blend of witch hazel and goosegrease, much better than any commercial stuff." The dispensary was a small room tucked away between the infirmary and the kitchen. There was a pleasant scent of spices and on the kitchen table an old fashioned pestle and mortar.

"I shall smear this on and lend you a pair of thin cotton gloves. Wear them until the salve has soaked in, then come back this afternoon and I'll put more on for you. Did you take a header into a bramble bush?"

"It feels like that," Sister Joan said, submitting to the other's ministrations gratefully.

"It seems as if you've been here for ages, doesn't it?" Sister Perpetua was chattering. "I find it quite hard to realise you only arrived last Saturday. I do hope that things are going to go well now, if you know what I mean?"

"Do you feel better about things?" Sister Joan said bluntly.

"Oh yes," Sister Perpetua assured her. "My neuralgia is really improving."

As Sister Joan stared at her in astonishment Sister Felicity said from the doorway.

"I have to go into Bodmin this morning. Shall I buy some feed for Lilith?"

"That would be very kind of you, Sister," Sister Joan said, turning slightly.

"Have you hurt your hands, Sister?" Sister Felicity looked concerned.

"Nothing very serious," Sister Perpetua said. "Sister Joan must wear gloves when she rides Lilith in future."

"I'll get on then." The lay sister gave her broad smile and stomped out.

"I didn't wish to reveal my own worries," Sister Perpetua whispered. "They will only tell me that it is imagination, my old trouble."

"Your old trouble?" Sister Joan glanced at her.

"I had a slight breakdown some years ago," Sister Perpetua said, looking embarrassed. "Not a really bad one. I didn't have to go into hospital or anything like that. Just shock after an unfortunate—oh my! That's Sister Andrew wanting another cup of coffee. Excuse me."

She scurried out, her reddish eyebrows working furiously.

A breakdown? Nuns did occasionally have breakdowns, usually at the menopause when it dawned on them that there was now no possibility even if they did the unthinkable and left the religious life, of their bearing children. Most of them didn't even want children let alone husbands but their bodies betrayed them into useless regrets. Perhaps it had been like that with Sister Perpetua. Perhaps it would be like that with herself. She pushed the morbid thought away and went out to the stable to saddle up Lilith.

This morning the rain had stopped. The night had been dry too, she recalled. Perhaps summer was really on the way. Solstice certainly was. She would have to sit down and work out where everything fitted before long, but for the moment she had better concentrate on the lessons she intended to give that morning.

This morning two of the farm children were absent.

" 'Tis plague, Sister," one of the other children informed her sadly, when she made enquiry.

"Plague?" Sister Joan stared at them.

"Yes, Sister, chickenpox plague," he said. "They'm mortal bad."

"Chickenpox." She cast a swift look round those who had turned up. "In that case it might be a good idea if those of you who haven't had chickenpox stayed at home for a few days."

The suggestion was not well received which was flattering when she thought about it. In any case if any of them had been infected it had probably happened by now.

With some difficulty she got them down to their reading books, feeling a tinge of annoyance when she saw that in the pictures that sprinkled the pages of their Primary Readers the father was the one who drove the lorry and gave the orders while the mother made the birthday cake and picked flowers. She would have to find out who supplied the textbooks and see if more up-to-date ones could be bought.

The morning passed fairly peacefully. These were basically nice children, she thought, who might be fated to spend their lives following the furrow their parents and grandparents had ploughed but were nonetheless bright and lively. If she could impress upon one of them that the world was moving on it would be worth while.

"Don't bother to tell me that bullshit about the equality of the sexes again," Jacob had said angrily, "when you're running away from any competition with men by burying yourself alive among a pack of sex-starved women.''

"I will give you a pound for every sex-starved nun you can produce,'' she'd said. ''And that doesn't mean they're all indulging in orgies behind convent walls either.''

She had known even then that it was not cowardice or a broken heart that pulled her towards the cloister. She loved Jacob, would in some part of herself always love him, and having known his loving she must protect herself against bitterness by transmitting that physical experience into something spiritual.

A wry grin touched her lips at the direction of her thoughts. Five years before she had been impossibly idealistic, striking mental attitudes all over the place. If anyone had told her then that the deprivation she would feel most was not sex but the freedom to walk for hours with no bell or Novice Mistress to recall her she would have been astonished.

The morning gone she dismissed the children with instructions to stay at home if they felt sick and watched Johnny Russell's form materialise from a clump of heather.

"You didn't sleep there all night, did you?'' she asked, amused, as he came striding up.

"About half an hour,'' he said. ''Is that your lunch?''

In the act of taking the flask of coffee and the Cornish pasty out of the saddle bag where Sister Margaret had put them, she said gracefully,

"Our lunch. I'll drink the coffee and you can eat the pasty. I'm not keen.''

"Is that true, or are you practising unselfishness?'' he asked suspiciously.

"It happens to be true,'' she assured him. ''Come into the schoolroom. What did you find out?''

"The Prioress rang Mrs. Williams and told her that
Brenda had left the convent and was on a commune in
Wales," he told her, biting into the pasty. "When I
rang up she started telling me about it right off, asking
if I knew anything, wondering why she hadn't gone
home. I didn't tell her that I was down here."

"Did you manage to get hold of a copy of the inquest
report?"

"In the Public Library," he said, turning to open his
backpack. "They have everything on video now, but
the assistant gave me a print out. There isn't much
there." The account was succinct, evidently written by
a local reporter who'd been told not to sensationalise.

"The Coroner returned a verdict of Death by Misadventure yesterday on Sister Sophia Brentwood, of the
Order of the Daughters of Compassion, whose death
was reported in this newspaper a week ago, and whose
funeral took place yesterday. The delay in the funeral
was caused by the autopsy ordered by the Chief Con-
stable upon the body."

"The police evidently thought there was something
fishy about her death," Johnny pointed out as she
marked the place with her finger and frowned.

"Reverend Mother Ann Gillespie testified that she
and one of the lay sisters had gone to the convent chapel
to undertake a meditation and that Sister Sophia had
joined them. They had been discussing fire-safety pre-
cautions earlier and decided that it might be a good idea
to test the apparatus. Sister Sophia volunteered because
of her youth and greater mobility to be the guinea-pig
and went up to her cell on the first floor of the convent
to test it. Unfortunately the strap which was designed
to go under one arm and over one shoulder was worn
and slippery and as Sister Sophia was attaching the
hooks to the sill the arm strap slipped around her neck.
Reverend Mother Ann Gillespie testified that Sister So-

phia who had begun to lower herself from the window fell as the strap tightened. She had no time to call out or lever herself back over the sill. Mother Ann and the Lay Sister, Felicity Brown, immediately ran indoors and raised their companion but she was not conscious. Sister Felicity then telephoned for the doctor and roused Sister Perpetua Fielding who is Infirmarian in the convent. All attempts to revive Sister Sophia failed. Sister Felicity Brown confirmed the evidence given by Mother Ann Gillespie and a signed statement from Sister Perpetua Fielding who is still suffering from shock was read out and confirmed previous evidence.

"Dr. Mansell Tudor testified that he was called out to the convent at five past eleven in the evening and reached the convent fifteen minutes later. He had delayed only to phone for an ambulance which arrived five minutes after he himself had reached the scene. He had applied mouth-to-mouth resuscitation without success and had cooperated with the medical staff in the ambulance in the application of shock treatment used for emergencies, but all vital signs were lacking. The strap was so tight round Sister Sophia's neck that it had to be cut away, and in his opinion the sudden tightening of the said strap combined with the dead weight of Sister Sophia as she fell from the window had killed her instantaneously.

"Mr. Justice Penrhyn, District Coroner, then gave his verdict, adding a rider which deplored the careless use of apparatus already out of date and in a faulty condition."

"I wonder why the police wanted an autopsy," Sister Joan said thoughtfully.

"I thought of that myself," Johnny said triumphantly, "so I went and asked."

"That was enterprising!" She gave him an approving look.

"Well, I didn't actually go to the police station," he said. "I thought that it might look a bit peculiar if I started asking questions about a nun I never even knew. I went to the local pub and hung around there, just listening and dropping in the odd question now and then. They don't open up much to strangers, but I sort of hinted that I'd relatives in a convent—not an outright lie, honest, since Brenda would have been related to me if we'd got married—anyway the men in the bar started talking about Sister Sophia's death. One of them said his cousin was in the local police and the police thought the whole matter was a bit peculiar, so there was an autopsy but they didn't find anything wrong."

Which knocked on the head any possibility that Sister Sophia had suffered from epilepsy.

"Sister, what are we going to do now?" He had finished the pasty and was regarding her gravely. "I don't think the death of the other nun had anything to do with Brenda leaving the convent. Do you know exactly when she did leave?"

"On the sixteenth of February," Sister Joan said. "Sister Felicity drove her to the station and saw her on to the train."

Johnny consulted the bold-faced watch on his wrist and announced,

"That was a Tuesday. I could ask around, find out if a nun had got on the train—"

"No, she'd have been in the clothes she came in," Sister Joan broke in. "They are kept until she completes her period in the Novitiate. If a novice leaves, her convent dress and bonnet are kept for the next novice. It sometimes results in rather odd fits, but it all helps to discourage vanity—how tall is Brenda?"

"Five eight, quite bosomy," Johnny said and blushed.

Veronica Stirling was only about five feet five inches

and slender. The dress handed on to her would have been altered by Sister Katherine who was in charge of linen.

"Go and see what you can find out at the station then." She reverted to the original subject.

"Is there something odd going on at the convent then?" he demanded.

Sister Joan hesitated, wondering exactly how to explain the situation to someone not reared in Catholic tradition without sounding absurdly mediaeval.

"Life in any convent," she said at last, "has certain features that would strike any lay person as odd. They did me when I entered the Novitiate and I'd been a Catholic all my life. The Daughters of Compassion is a modern Order, founded less than fifty years ago, and yet in many ways it remains very traditional. Each convent is independent for all practical purposes but the rules as laid down by our founder remain constant though in small ways each prioress interprets them according to her own wishes. But the spirit of the rules is always kept. I mean one prioress might agree to let the novices join in some particular spiritual exercise with the rest of the Community or allow one of the professed nuns to receive a telephone call, but no prioress would allow any of her nuns to wear lipstick or go out dancing in the local disco. It would be against the spirit of the rules."

"Is that what the prioress here does?" Johnny asked with interest.

"No, of course not, but she wears pink nail varnish and perfumes her clothes, which is perfectly all right for a laywoman to do but not for a nun who's put away worldly vanities. And then the novices here—I have discovered their heads are not shaven; their hair is not even cut short."

"Is your hair—?" Johnny looked inquisitive.

"About two inches long all over and apt to curl," Sister Joan said with a grin. "But then I am now fully professed and supposed to be better able to handle personal vanity. As one progresses further in the religious life so the rules become slightly less stringent, but never for the novices."

"Who chooses the prioress?" he asked.

"She is elected by the professed nuns," Sister Joan explained. "Her term of office lasts for five years and she is not allowed to serve more than two consecutive terms. Once a nun has served as prioress she is known as Mother instead of Sister. It must all seem rather petty and silly to you."

"A bit like being in school," he admitted. "But you do get out, don't you? To teach, I mean?"

"In our Order those sisters who can earn their living are encouraged to do so. Each of our convents is self-supporting. That doesn't relieve me of my religious duties, by the bye. I must still attend services and prayers and group meditation."

"On Sundays?" he asked.

"Every day," she said firmly, and smothered a giggle at the look on his face. "In fact we rise at five and spend two hours in chapel before breakfast. In the late afternoon we spend a further two hours at religious studies or meditation, and that doesn't include private prayer."

She broke off abruptly, mentally scolding herself for showing off, but her companion was clearly unimpressed.

"I told Brenda she was an idiot to go and tie herself down in a convent," he said. "No offence, Sister."

"None taken," she said gracefully. "Look, I have to go. I honestly don't feel there's much more that I can find out about Brenda. However I'll give it another couple of days."

"I'll make some enquiries at the station. The other nun would have seen her off?"

"Sister Felicity, yes. There are two Lay Sisters in each convent who share most of the cooking and cleaning, deal with the outside world and so on. They are excused some of the meditation periods. Sister Felicity is bound to be known. She drives an old car of which she is very proud; big, country-type woman, rather jolly."

"I'll see you tomorrow then, Sister," he said.

"Yes—no, I won't be here tomorrow. Sister David is coming in instead. I'll be back on Friday morning."

"Is it any use trying to find out anything?" His face was suddenly sombre. "Honestly Sister, I get the impression that we're just going round in circles."

Sister Joan, who had begun to feel that way herself, promptly began to feel differently.

"If you are sure that Brenda would have gone straight home when she left the convent then that is what she probably would have done, since you obviously knew her very well," she said firmly. "What I want to find out is why she left and if it had anything to do with Sister Sophia's death. I'll see you on Friday, Johnny."

Locking up after he had strode off she wondered what on earth would happen if they could find out nothing more or if Brenda didn't get in touch with her parents.

Letting the mare pick her way lazily down the track she tried to fit together the disparate pieces of the puzzle. The laxity of the rules in Cornwall House, the worries of old Sister Frances, the death of Sister Sophia, the sudden departure of Brenda who had been Sister Magdalen. It really was like a puzzle, she reflected, but she was trying to solve it without any guiding picture to help her decide where each separate piece fitted. And there was always the possibility that her instincts were wrong, that the only thing wrong at the convent was that the Prioress had unconventional notions, that Sister Sophia had merely slipped and fallen, and that Brenda had simply walked out of the Novitiate and gone off to a commune in Wales because she wanted time alone to sort out her desires.

A small car was being driven at a snail's pace behind her. She guided Lilith on to the turf as the car drew alongside and Father Malone stuck his greying head out of the window.

"Good day to you, Sister," he said genially. "On your way back from the school?"

"Yes, Father." She dismounted politely.

"And how are you settling at Cornwall House now?" he wanted to know.

"I'm finding my feet," she said cautiously.

"You have a fine lot of examples there to inspire you," he said.

Startled, she looked at him, suspecting irony but he was sincere, continuing with enthusiasm.

"Reverend Mother Ann has a great devotion now to Our Blessed Lady. It's my belief that devotion to the Holy Mother is the backbone of our Faith."

Her initial impression of him had been correct. A good, simple man whose theology was naive.

"Devotion to Our Lord too," she said mildly.

"Of course, that goes without saying, but if Our Blessed Lady had not accepted the Will of God then Our Blessed Lord would never have been born at all," he said.

"But if Our Lady was perfect then She could not have refused," Sister Joan said. "I mean there would have been no conflict between her will and Divine Will."

"Exactly so, Sister! I can see you've a good head on your shoulders." He looked slightly confused.

"Are you on your way to the convent now, Father?" she asked, somewhat unnecessarily since there was no other building in that direction. "I hope nothing's wrong?"

"Wednesday afternoon, Sister. Confession for those sisters who require it. What were you thinking might be wrong? There's no sickness at the convent, is there?"

"I was thinking about Sister Sophia," she risked saying. "I've been hearing about the accident."

"A terrible tragedy indeed," he concurred. "That poor young sister! Ah, but it was very foolish to go testing the apparatus at that late hour. Reverend Mother Ann was devastated. Now there is a splendid woman for you, Sister. She looks upon the sisters as her own daughters and this is a woman who might have had a distinguished worldly career. Her father was a most famous man. It'll be a grand day when she publishes his notes and writings that he left behind when he was taken from us."

He raised his hand in blessing and started up the car again.

Whatever was going on at Cornwall House had nothing to do with Father Malone, Sister Joan thought, gazing after the car. It was clear that he was a good simple man dazzled by Reverend Mother Ann's superior intellect. She was more certain than ever that nobody had ever invited him to one of the talks on pagan goddesses.

She reached the stable without seeing anyone else, unsaddled Lilith and gave her some of the feed from the large sack of it that Sister Felicity had evidently left.

She would give Confession a miss, she decided, since at this moment it would be impossible for her to make a completely full and frank one. Meanwhile she could have a quiet word with Sister Katherine.

She found the latter in the recreation room, cutting out quantities of green cotton.

"Costumes for the local children at Solstice," Sister Katherine said, glancing up with a smile. "They are going to be woodland piskies. There's a very nice procession and a bazaar and dancing in the streets. The whole festival was in danger of dying out until Grant Tarquin was elected to the Council and decided to revive it. After all Helston has the Furry Dance, so it seems only fair that Bodmin should have something too.''

"Would you like some help?" Sister Joan sat down and picked up a swathe of green.

"If you could cut fringes into these and sew up the sides. They're just tubes really with holes for head and limbs. That would be a big help."

"I feel a bit of a fraud," Sister Joan confessed, taking scissors and cotton. "Preparing lessons certainly doesn't take the whole afternoon."

"Sister Sophia used to say that," Sister Katherine said. "She used to accuse herself of being lazy."

"Was she?"

"Heavens no. She always worked very hard. The days weren't long enough she used to say. She was so excited when she made her final profession."

"But she was slightly depressed later on, wasn't she?"

"Was she?" Sister Katherine looked surprised. "I suppose she was a bit quiet, now I come to think of it. But that's natural, don't you think? I made my final profession two years ago and it was quite a shock to wake up the next morning and find out that I hadn't grown wings and halo. I dare say that Sister Katherine is going to remain plain old Sister Katherine to the end of the story."

"Were you in the Novitiate at the same time?"

"As Sister Sophia? No, I was coming into the Community as she was entering. She was a couple of years younger than I was."

"And Reverend Mother Ann was Prioress?"

"Ever since Cornwall House was opened she and Mother Frances, God rest her soul, have been elected turn and turn about," Sister Katherine said. "This is Reverend Mother Ann's second turn of office though so I cannot think who we will elect next time. Reverend Mother is such a brilliant woman."

"She has some unconventional ideas certainly," Sister Joan said mildly.

"To be perfectly honest," Sister Katherine confided, "I don't really understand all that she says, though it is most interesting. Of course since Vatican Two many ideas are changing quite drastically. I'm afraid my talents lie in my fingers rather than my head."

"Considerable talents surely if what I've glimpsed of your work so far is anything to go by."

"Oh, what a nice thing to say." Sister Katherine's plain little face beamed. "I was always very fond of needlework and my embroidered altar cloths and copes bring in quite a lot for the convent. Someone mentioned you were artistic yourself, Sister Joan?"

"I had hopes of becoming a professional once," Sister Joan said, "until I discovered that my ambitions exceeded my gifts. Then I settled for being a first-rate teacher (that is hopefully) rather than a second-rate portrait painter."

"Perhaps you could make portraits of some of the sisters for jubilee or final profession?" Sister Katherine suggested. "They would be more unusual than photographs and some of the novices look so pretty on their profession day."

"Cornwall House seems to go in for pretty novices."

"Only in the last year or so," Sister Katherine said. "It happens like that sometimes, I dare say. Not that physical beauty is supposed to matter but one cannot avoid noticing it. You should have seen Sister Magdalen. She was the loveliest girl."

"She left, didn't she?" Sister Joan snipped away at a fringe.

"In the middle of February," Sister Katherine nodded. "Not that I ever had much to do with her, of course, but she helped out shortly after her arrival when we had the influenza epidemic. A very sweet, happy girl. I was surprised when I heard she had left."

"You saw her leave?"

"No, but then when a novice leaves she usually does so when most of the Community are in chapel as you know," Sister Katherine said, adding with a giggle, "I have often wondered why. Perhaps they think we will all follow the bad example and run out after her."

"At least her leaving gave you an extra task," Sister Joan said. "Altering her novice dress to fit the next newcomer, I mean."

Sister Katherine frowned slightly as if a thought previously thrust down had reared up again. After a moment she said,

"Actually I was not required to make any alteration. Perhaps there was a spare dress that fitted the new novice better."

"As Linen Mistress you would know."

"Yes, one would think so," Sister Katherine said, her tone still troubled, "but the truth is that I don't, you see."

TWELVE

✠ ✠ ✠

"As you are not going to school today," Reverend Mother Ann said at breakfast the next morning, "perhaps you would like to go over to the Novitiate, Sister Joan?"

Sister Joan, sipping her morning coffee, jumped slightly, wondering if the Prioress was telepathic since she had been trying to think up a way to get into the Novitiate for hours, within a single idea coming into her head. Apart from services in chapel and the general confession once a week the novices were secluded as rigidly as if they all had the plague.

"Certainly, Reverend Mother?" She let her voice rise into a question.

"Sister Katherine was telling Mother Emmanuel of her idea that portraits of the novices might be painted and Mother Emmanuel considered it an excellent idea," the Prioress said. "Of course none are near making their profession yet, but little portraits of them might give their families pleasure, don't you think?"

It was on the tip of Sister Joan's tongue to retort that that depended on the quality of the portraits, but that would have displayed pride. It was not for a nun to evaluate her own gifts. And it was a marvellous opportunity.

"I'll do my best, Reverend Mother," she said. "Would you want charcoal or watercolour?"

"Perhaps you could make sketches and work them up into watercolour portraits later," the other said. "You know in the Novitiate it is considered vital that the personality be refined and honed to come closer to the ideal, and it occurred to me that such portraits in revealing certain traits for good or ill might be a spiritual help to the girls."

"I am not an experienced portrait-artist," Sister Joan felt bound to point out. "I can catch a likeness, that's all."

"We will not expect more," Reverend Mother Ann said pleasantly. "You will not of course converse with the novices while you are there."

"No, Reverend Mother." Bowing, retreating from the dining-room, Sister Joan resisted the urge to give a hop, skip and jump. Even without conversation it might be possible to find out a great deal.

She collected her materials and stepped out briskly, waving to Sister David who was on the way down the drive. Lilith would have to do without her exercise today.

The morning was cool and damp, with a faint scent of violets in the air. There would be clumps of them deep in the woods beyond the moor, she thought, and late bluebells with the darker streaks on their petals fading to white when they were plucked. On the moor tangles of meadowsweet would trail lace over the green bracken and the first purple of heather would spread itself in the hollows. She would have liked to walk in the cool of woods and moor, her ankle length skirt tucked up, her head bare, She savoured the wish for a moment or two, then went smilingly round the corner to the old tennis-court. Sister Hilaria was at the door of the Novitiate, her eyes fixing themselves on Sister Joan's approaching figure with a look in them of surprise though she had been standing near when the Prioress had made her request.

"Good morning, Sister Hilaria." Sister Joan raised her voice slightly. "I am to make sketches of the novices."

"Yes. Of course." Sister Hilaria gave her vague, slightly distracted smile. "They are here somewhere. It is a question of rounding them up. You'll want them one at a time?" She spoke as if they were wild ponies to be corralled instead of young girls under obedience.

"That would be splendid, Sister," Sister Joan said.

"If you will come into the recreation room," Sister Hilaria said, standing aside.

She had almost forgotten the atmosphere of a Novitiate, but it rushed back as she entered the narrow hallway with the steps rising to the upper floor. What struck her most as it had struck her when entering her own Novitiate for the first time was the complete lack of any colours save black and white and grey.

"In training the physical world must be narrowed down," her Novice Mistress said, "in preparation for the time when you finally renounce the world."

Here, as there, were small rooms, tiny windows covered with thick white nets, bare wooden floors, whitewashed walls, naked light bulbs. Sensual loveliness was banished here. In the recreation room a semicircle of stools and a long table were all the furniture.

"I will send them in, Sister," the Novice Mistress said.

"I will require more light," Sister Joan said, looking round with a measuring eye.

"Oh dear," Sister Hilaria looked flustered. "You

could pull back the curtains but I don't know what Mother Emmanuel will say.''

''Since you are Novice Mistress there isn't much she can say,'' Sister Joan said briskly.

''I suppose not.'' The other still seemed unhappy. ''Well, do what you feel is necessary, Sister. I'll just go and—''

She drifted out again, not completing her sentence.

Sister Joan went to the windows and pulled back each net, letting the pale, greyish light flood in. Cool, clean light, she thought, lifting her palms briefly to it.

''The novices are not to see the portraits,'' Sister Hilaria said, returning. With her was the white-skinned grey-eyed girl whose hair the Prioress had ruffled.

''And not to talk to me. I know.'' Sister Joan smiled at the girl who stood shyly, her hands clasped at the waist of her pale blue habit. The brim of the white bonnet hid any traces of hair and cast a soft shadow over commonplace features.

''This is Teresa,'' Sister Hilaria said.

''Sit down, Teresa.'' Sister Joan placed a chair where the light fell most strongly and herself took an opposite chair, settling herself with sketch-pad and thick soft pencil. Sister Hilaria had seated herself at the table and was gazing at the crucifix on the wall with eyes that looked as if they wished to see nothing else. Sister Joan suspected that she would not have heard one word if the other two had sung duets. It was a nuisance being vowed to obedience, she thought crossly, especially since this silence was the result of a direct order that couldn't be circumvented. Then her irritation faded as her fingers, gripping the pencil, began to move in lines and curves, pausing to shade and then moving on. She had not lost her skill, too slight ever to bring her fame, but indisputably there, as she drew the head and shoulders of Sister Teresa. She would have liked to ask questions. When a subject began to talk, to open out, the portrait became stronger, more revealing. On the other hand it was an interesting challenge to catch a likeness in silence, to portray a hint of stupidity in the slant of the eyes, an undeveloped sexuality in the full lower lip.

"Sister Hilaria?" Half an hour had passed and the sketch was as complete as she could make it. She had scribbled name and details of colouring on the back ready for the translation into watercolours to delight some proud family.

"Sister Joan?" The Novice Mistress blinked as if she were surfacing briefly from a heavy sleep.

"The sketch is finished. May another of the novices come in?"

"Sister Teresa, tell Rose to come down," she said.

"Yes, Sister. Thank you, Sister Joan." The novice bobbled a curtsy and went out. Barely a minute elapsed before a plump novice with a round face and the innocent mischief of a Botticelli angel in her blue eyes came in.

The same ritual was gone through. Sister Rose sat obediently in the shaft of light that came through the window; Sister Joan gripped a freshly sharpened pencil; Sister Hilaria resumed her contemplation of the crucifix.

This girl had more personality in her face, Sister Joan reflected, striving to capture the play of light and shade over the pert, mobile features. She wondered if it would be sufficiently suppressed to enable her to settle down in the religious life but privately doubted it. The mischief and humour would bubble forth at inconvenient moments. Sister Rose was succeeded by Sister Barbara who was thin and small and already conducted herself like a miniature prioress, hands folded, eyes downcast so that it was difficult to catch any glimpse of their colour.

Sister Joan's hand was beginning to ache slightly. Rubbing it she hoped that Sister Hilaria might offer a cup of tea and a respite, but Sister Hilaria sat still at the table, her brooding gaze on the crucifix, a woman who had left bodily needs behind her and forgot that others hadn't. Sister Hilaria would obey every command without question but she would notice nothing that threatened to intrude into her spiritual raptures. Sister Joan could almost hear Reverend Mother Agnes's wry comment.

"A truly elevated soul, and no convent can endure more than one such."

Veronica Stirling came in. She had brought a glass of lemonade which she set at Sister Joan's elbow with the polite bob she had learned in the few days since her arrival.

"Thank you, Sister Veronica." Sister Joan nodded her gratitude and drank thirstily.

Veronica had paused to look at the three sketches laid on the table. None of the others had so much as glanced at them. Veronica had not yet begun to learn custody of the eyes, it seemed, Sister Joan thought, and felt a distinct tendency to cheer loudly. She drained the lemonade and motioned the other to the chair, picking up sketch-pad and new pencil. The light was strengthening now, edged with the faint lemon of a struggling sun. It bathed the exquisite face of the novice who sat, dutifully silent, her fingers clutching the small crucifix at her sash.

Clutching? Sister Joan recognised the word, examined it, let her eyes move up to the pale, pretty face with the long-lashed blue eyes. Under the brim of the white bonnet the other's features seemed smaller and tighter than when she had chattered on the train. Was she nervous at having her portrait done? It seemed unlikely, yet there was a nervous quality about her, something fugitive and desperate that peeped out now and then from the tip of the tongue flicking round the inside of the unpainted mouth, the almost clawlike grip of the fingers on the little crucifix. What ailed the girl? Sister Joan wanted to reach out, taking the clutching fingers in her own, to say something light and reassuring, but physical contact between professed nuns was kept to a minimum. Between nuns and novices it was absolutely forbidden. And she was under orders to be silent. She was not, however, under orders not to use any facial gestures. She raised her head from the sketch-pad, flashed a cheerful grin and slowly and deliberately winked. Sister Veronica sent her an anguished glance and went paler than before. There was nothing to be done but draw steadily, softening the anguish into a smooth and meaningless expression that would have graced a chocolate box nicely.

"All finished." She spoke with the kind of heartiness she hated in other people. Veronica rose, glanced towards the sketches on the table, bobbed her curtsy and withdrew. Piling the sketches together Sister Joan wondered if she might not mention to Sister Hilaria that Veronica seemed troubled, but that would be an intrusion into private territory. Novice Mistresses were supposed to be on the alert for that kind of thing. A good Novice Mistress knew if one of her charges was unhappy before the novice herself became aware of it. Sister Hilaria might be a holy soul, Sister Joan thought with exasperation, but she was the most unsuitable guide for embryo religious that could possibly be imagined.

"Thank you very much, Sister."

Even raising her voice higher didn't help. Sister Hilaria's face was entranced; her eyes devoured the tortured figure on the crucifix with a hunger that was almost animal. Too much religious feeling was worse than too little, Sister Joan decided, putting the two chairs back into place and unlooping the nets. The cool, sun-rimmed light became ivory.

She picked up her things and went out quickly, closing the door, standing for a moment in the narrow corridor while she struggled with temptation.

No, it was no justification to say that the sketching being done she was released from her silence. Having reached that conclusion she turned in at the open door of the small library where volumes considered safe reading for girls under instruction were ranged. At that instant she had nothing more in her mind than the impulse to glance at the books on the shelves. They were, as might have been expected, standard fare with lives of the Saints jostling *The Interior Castle* and *The Little Flower*. A photograph of the Foundress hung on the wall between two netted windows; there were a couple of benches and a modest table with writing-paper, pens and notebooks on it. The door of a low cupboard in the corner swung open, key still in the lock, with a pile of notebooks on top. It was apparent that Sister Hilaria had been interrupted in her task of putting the notebooks away.

It was certainly none of her business what the notebooks contained. Sister Joan told herself, and went on telling herself while her hands sorted through the pile. Black covers with the names of past novices written on white slips of paper gummed to the front.

Sister Magdalen's Spiritual Diary was fifth from the top. Sister Joan extracted it, thrust the other notebooks inside the cupboard, turned the key and feeling as if she had just robbed a bank left the Novitiate.

Her next task was to find a secluded spot where she could peruse the notebook without fear of discovery. Even while she headed for the orchard where the leafy branches were concealing she was arguing herself into condoning her action. The notebook had no present relevance since its owner had left the convent; the maxim that the end justified the means was Jesuitical in the first place; she was not looking into it out of idle curiosity but because a decent young man was worried about the whereabouts of his friend.

She stopped beneath the gnarled branches of a wide-spreading apple tree, bunching up her skirts into the traditional cushion and lowering herself to grass that felt dry enough to leave no betraying stain. Staring at the book she reminded herself that she was doing this out of duty, admitted to herself that she was consumed with purely secular curiosity, and opened the book.

The writing was neat and round, the hand of a docile pupil who knows someone else is going to read it. The entries were not long and most of them were conventional expressions of joy at entering the Novitiate and of hopes she would be able to reach the required standard, interspersed with copious quotations from various religious texts. It was all entirely expected and rather dull.

"I am feeling a bit homesick and must remember that detachment is a virtue for which I must constantly strive. My parents are often in my mind, but in two years' time I will see them on the happy day I take my first vows. Despite my moments of depression I feel strongly that I have chosen the right life."

There were references to the influenza epidemic.

"It is a real privilege to be able to help out in the Infirmary, Mother Frances is an astonishing old lady. She is past ninety and physically frail now but her mind is clear as a bell. She has been a nun since she was eighteen, and is a marvellous example to the rest of us."

Her initial homesickness seemed to have worn off rapidly. By the first week in November she was writing,

"Now that the 'flu seems to have run its course we can concentrate on our spiritual duties. I had never real-

ised before the excitement and beauty of the religious
life. Reverend Mother Ann has had several private talks
with me, and her words are both inspiring and terrify-
ing. She is, of course, a woman of great vision and
courage who will take the Order forward into the
twenty-first century. I only pray that I am worthy of
such confidence.'' And that was all. The remaining
pages showed that at least a dozen had been carefully
torn out, only the loose threads of the inner binding
revealing the fact.

Sister Joan sat back on her heels and decided to stop
feeling guilty about being inquisitive. Sister Magdalen
nee Brenda Williams had been a starry-eyed, somewhat
naïve girl who had evidently settled down well in the
Novitiate, had helped out cheerfully during the influenza epidemic, had struggled successfully against her
very natural homesickness, and had been determined to
make a good profession. Everything written in the book
merely confirmed the opinions everybody else had given
of her, but the missing pages which presumably filled
in the weeks between the beginning of November and
the sixteenth of February might well take a very different complexion. And her novice's dress had not been
altered for Veronica. That might mean nothing. It was
possible there had been a spare outfit nearer to the new
novice's size. The other dress and bonnet might be in
some cupboard somewhere, and Sister Katherine had
simply forgotten about it. Sister Joan pictured the other's plain, sensible young face, the neat stitches she had
been taking in the costumes for the Solstice's fete, and
thought it unlikely. Sister Katherine, Sister Martha and
Sister David were conscientious but not particularly intellectual sisters who kept the rules, worshipped in the
simple, unquestioning way of their forebears and never
saw what was not pushed under their noses. Whatever
was going on beneath the placid routine of conventual

life was known only to a selected few of the sisters, she reflected. The Prioress must be the instigator, Mother Emmanuel and Sister Felicity and Sister Lucy were her accomplices—the word entered her mind unbidden and refused to be changed into something less sinister.

Was it possible that Sister Perpetua was right and that Sister Sophia had been driven to take her own life in the same way that Sister Magdalen had been driven to leave so abruptly? If she had left. Those four words also sprang unwanted into her mind and refused to go away. She hoped fervently that Johnny would have been given confirmation of his friend's leaving on the train. Then whatever had led her to leave so suddenly might not be as terrible as she was beginning to fear.

"The point is," she muttered, "that I haven't the slightest notion what it is I do fear."

She had not yet taken a second look at the sketches of the novices. Closing the notebook and resolving to return it as soon as any opportunity arose she slid the drawings out of the cardboard file and examined them closely.

"One thing you always contrive to do," Jacob had said, "is catch the personality of your subject. Your technique is abominable but you manage to show more than you realise, you know, when you're doing the work."

"That makes my work glib," she had complained.

"Also perceptive." He had spoken without envy, secure in the knowledge that his own gifts were superior.

Sister Teresa had a lively face, a smile lurking at the corners of the full mouth, the grey eyes wide and intelligent. A possible future prioress, Sister Joan thought. She must remember when she came to paint the watercolours that the skin had that thick whiteness that sometimes goes with red hair.

Sister Rose had a genuine sweetness in her face. In

feature she was not dissimilar to Sister Lucy with her heart-shaped bone structure and slanting eyes, but Sister Lucy was like a shy little cat with claws ready to wound. Sister Rose was a kitten.

Sister Barbara's face revealed nothing beyond the docility of a girl already resigned to perpetual obedience. Either she was too dull to struggle or too high-minded. Sister Joan wondered if anyone would ever find out which. Probably not even Sister Barbara knew. She had kept the last until last partly because having travelled down with Veronica she felt a certain interest in her and partly because the girl's altered looks had alarmed her.

She had not betrayed it in the sketch with its placid eyes and grave expression, but the sketch was no more than a pretty mask for the Prioress to approve.

From the unused sheets of paper a small piece fluttered down.

She read its message as she picked it up.

"Dear Sister Joan,

"Can you meet me after general confession in the stable? I think I can make an excuse to slip away. Please do come. Something is worrying me very much and I need your advice.

"Yours sincerely,
"Veronica Stirling."

Not Yours in Christ or Sister Veronica. This was a cry for help from a girl with whom she had shared an uneventful journey, a girl whose enthusiasm and excitement had been changed into fear.

On Fridays the usual recreation in the Order was replaced by the general confession in which professed nuns and novices made public confession of their faults. In some Orders it was also the practice for the sisters to confess faults they had noticed in others, but the

Foundress had been emphatic in her disapproval of that practice.

''Let each Daughter of Compassion seek out her own sins and leave others to do the same'' was written in the Guide to Conduct upon which her first convent had been founded. Sister Joan, contemplating ways in which she could sneak off for an unauthorised meeting with one of the novices, thought wryly that her own list of misdemeanours was now so alarmingly long that she would certainly have had no time to pay heed to the sins of anyone else.

THIRTEEN

✠ ✠ ✠

"You have a pleasant rest today, Sister?"

The Prioress had spoken to her at Recreation with a smiling lilt in her voice.

"Such a pleasant one that I am feeling guilty of sloth," Sister Joan had replied. "I hope you are not too wearied, Sister David?"

"Oh, I enjoyed being with the children again," Sister David assured her. "This morning we rehearsed the songs and dances for the Solstice festival. They are the same from year to year but the children forget them. Perhaps we might agree to let me take over from you every Thursday."

"Certainly, if Reverend Mother—?"

"You have permission to arrange the school rota as you choose," the Prioress said, inclining her head slightly. "With your skill at drawing, Sister Joan, you might think of painting for cards and calendars. That would be a lucrative sideline for the convent."

"If I can't be a great artist I won't be an artist," she had said passionately once to Jacob.

"Yes, of course," she said now, and was surprised to find herself looking forward to the prospect of holding brushes and canvases again, even if the finished products would not hang in the Tate Gallery. "But you have not judged my sketches yet."

"When are we to see them?" Mother Emmanuel enquired. "The girls were telling me that you work very rapidly and professionally."

"We shall see the finished watercolours," the Prioress said. "No work of art should be unveiled until it is complete and perfect. I myself would have collated and published my father's final notes long since had I not determined to translate them to the best of my ability."

"Your father didn't work in English?" Sister Joan asked.

"He used a code of his own based on the Hittite script," the other answered. "In the field of archaeology I regret to say there are those who steal the work of others and present it as their own. My father was working on certain Aramaic documents when he died, and some years ago I began the massive task of transliterating them from the code he used into English and then into Latin."

"It will be a real feather in the Order's cap when the work appears in print," Mother Emmanuel said.

"All work is for the glory of God," the Prioress said reproachfully, "but it is true that the published scripts may well set the name of the Order in ecclesiastical history." She had nodded smilingly at the other and Mother Emmanuel had smiled back, her eyes raised in one brief, flashing glance of triumph.

Now, waiting for Johnny Russell to arrive, Sister Joan wondered what had occasioned the nodding and smiling. Thinking of the Community she saw them as a series of concentric circles radiating out from the elegant figure of Reverend Mother Ann.

The smallest inner circle consisted of Mother Emmanuel, Sister Lucy and Sister Felicity who were clearly part of whatever was going on. Beyond them she placed herself and Sister Perpetua, the shrouded figures of Sister Sophia and Mother Frances and Veronica. It was likely that Sister Magdalen/Brenda belonged there too. She saw them as each holding the solution to a piece of the puzzle but bewildered and separated. In the outermost circle were the other sisters, David, Katherine, Martha, Dorothy, Hilaria, Margaret and the three old ladies in the Infirmary.

It was difficult to fit in the other three novices since she knew nothing about them. She didn't even know which ones had been in the Novitiate when Brenda had left or when Sister Sophia had died. Perhaps others apart from Veronica were worried or perhaps they simply accepted everything that happened as she herself had accepted the discipline of the religious training.

"Good morning, Sister."

Johnny had put his head in at the door.

"Good morning. Come in, please."

His greeting had sounded cheerful enough but a closer look at his face revealed a sombre, brooding expression that sat oddly on his youthful features.

"She never left by train," he said abruptly before she could frame a question. "She never went on the train."

"How can you be so sure?" she demanded.

"I asked at the booking office," he told her. "I know it was back in February but there were fewer tourists then and they'd have remembered her, especially with a nun with her. I asked the clerk and the station master and they neither of them recall anyone from the convent seeing anyone off."

"That's hardly proof positive," she objected. "People do forget things, you now. It's possible that Sister Felicity didn't come on to the platform with her. Sister Magdalen—that's to say Brenda, might have had a return ticket and used that or had her ticket bought for her a couple of days previously. There are all sorts of possibilities."

Her voice trailed away as he shook his head.

"I just knew that something was wrong the minute you said she'd left," he said. "Look, I've known Brenda all her life. She didn't just rush into the convent in the first place. It did seem a bit like that to me but she'd obviously been thinking about it for a long time, and she's not a quitter, Sister Joan. Even if she was a bit disillusioned with being a novice she'd have stuck it out, and even if she did leave she would have gone home to see her parents. She wouldn't have run off to a commune."

"Her novice's dress wasn't handed down," Sister Joan said.

"What?" The young man looked at her.

"The novices wear pale blue dresses with white collars and white poke bonnets. If a novice leaves the Order or when she becomes a nun her novice dress is handed down to the next girl who enters. Alterations are made to fit the new girl. Brenda's dress wasn't handed in to the Linen Mistress."

"Could she have run away still wearing it?"

"She didn't need to run away," Sister Joan repeated patiently. "All she had to do was give one month's notice. Even if she dispensed with that and decided to walk out nobody would have compelled her to stay. The religious life is a voluntary one. Otherwise it has no value."

"Then she never left at all," Johnny said slowly.

"Well, she certainly isn't still in the—no, that's not possible." The thought was so grotesque that she was able to banish it at once. "Nothing has happened to her. For heaven's sake, this is a respectable convent. Nothing very exciting ever happens in convents." Except that one nun had died in a freak accident and an

old nun had written a letter that made no sense and a
novice had disappeared.

"I think I ought to go to the police," Johnny said.

"That's ridiculous!" Her face flushed as her tone
sharpened. "You seem to forget that she telephoned the
Prioress the other evening."

"She wouldn't have done that either," Johnny said
staunchly. "She'd have phoned home direct. Sorry, Sister Joan, but I don't trust your Prioress."

In one flashing thought Sister Joan rejected what he
had just said. The elegant woman with the polished
nails and the amused dark eyes was not "her" prioress.
Her prioress was tall and austere with honest eyes.

"You can't possibly go to the police yet," she said
aloud. "Brenda hasn't been reported as a missing person."

"I can do that."

"You're not a relative and you've no cause to believe
any crime has been committed. Look, I'm meeting the
new novice tonight, Veronica Stirling. She wishes to
speak to me privately, and it may well be that she can
throw some light on what's been happening. Give me
the weekend. If you haven't talked with Brenda by then
you can take what action you think is necessary."

For a moment she feared he was going to refuse.
Then he gave a reluctant nod.

"I'll be here on Monday," he said.

The words sounded like a threat, she reflected,
watching him stride away.

She was turning to lock up when the sound of a car
caused her to pause. The vehicle slowed and stopped
and Grant Tarquin wound down the window.

"Good morning, Sister. Is that young man still both-
ering you?" He sounded pleasantly concerned but his
eyes were sharp.

"Not at all. He seems to be enjoying his holiday," she rejoined. "Was there something you wanted?"

"From you? No, no, Sister. I was on my way elsewhere." He sounded amused now. "Did you have a satisfying first week? Teaching?"

He wasn't like Jacob at all. Jacob would have scorned innuendo.

"I found my feet," she said briskly. "The children have been coming regularly which is a hopeful sign. Sister David and I will divide the hours between us in the future. If you'll excuse me—?"

Turning the key, casting a last glance over the closed windows, she went over to Lilith and mounted up, humming under her breath. Had Jacob been there he would have enquired what was making her nervous.

"Have a pleasant weekend, Sister," Grant Tarquin called and drove off.

Trotting down the track Joan wondered if she would. Usually the weekend was a period towards which she looked forward eagerly throughout the week. The fasting from midday on Saturday until breakfast on Sunday emptied one of the week's troubles, made one feel lighter in mind and conscience, linked one to the other great religious Orders stretching back through the centuries. On Sunday the Low Mass of weekdays was replaced by the longer and more elaborate High Mass with its pure, asexual Gregorian chants. On Sundays letters home could be written, walks taken, the period of recreation doubled, enlivened by songs and the mild jests over which the religious had chuckled for generations.

Meanwhile she had to find a way of meeting Veronica Stirling in the stable after the general confession.

That problem occupied her mind during the afternoon while she marked the exercises the children had done during the week, drew up a rough timetable of projects to be done during the week to come and jotted down the faults she intended to confess. The list, she thought wryly, was a lot shorter than it ought to have been.

After supper and Benediction the nuns filed into the parlour. Even this was an innovation. In her old convent the general confession had been held in the dining-room with each nun rising in her place. Here the faded luxury of the surroundings made the idea of penance an alien thing.

Sister Hilaria came in, trailing three of the novices behind her as if she were in danger of forgetting them. Veronica had not been in her place at supper and Sister Hilaria said now in her vague fashion,

"Sister Veronica has a sick headache, Reverend Mother Ann, so I excused her from the meal and the general confession."

"Are my services required?" Sister Perpetua asked.

"She told me that she sleeps off a bad headache," Sister Hilaria said. "I understand she hardly ever suffers from them."

"If the sleep doesn't relieve it do call me." Sister Perpetua looked faintly disappointed at losing a patient.

"One only hopes she is not subject to them," Mother Emmanuel said irritably. "Some of these girls are apt to expect the novitiate to be one long holiday."

"Shall we begin, Sisters?" The Prioress looked round brightly.

Sister Joan concentrated her attention on her list of faults, trying to follow the advice her own Novice Mistress had given:

"Try to banish from your mind any personal likes or dislikes of the other Sisters you may have. Listen to the fault confessed, mentally bless the speaker, then forget it. When you leave the room leave your memory of faults confessed behind you."

It was not always easy advice to follow. She remembered with amusement one nun who had regularly confessed that she craved hamburgers more than anything else so that she had never been able to meet the other later without seeing her gazing soulfully at a large hamburger. The problem was that most of the faults were so predictable and so dull that the mind was apt to wander. This gathering was no exception. The others had all been tempted to stay in bed a couple of minutes longer than was allowed, to take a second helping, to have had the odd uncharitable thought or spoken thoughtlessly. Nobody had ever stood up and declared they had masturbated or worked out ways of slowly killing the Sister who belched after meals. Her own faults sounded like everybody else's. She had neglected to attend the priest's confession which, though attendance was voluntary, betokened less fervour than might be expected and she had forgotten to feed or groom Lilith.

"Twice!" she exclaimed, suddenly remembering. "I forgot about the poor creature today too." There was a ripple of stifled giggles interrupted by Reverend Mother Ann's amused voice. "Sister, I think you may be excused immediately in order that you may put the fault right."

"Yes, Reverend Mother." Sister Joan crossed herself, bowed to the Community and hurried out. It had not been a deliberate action on her part but now, at least, she had some excuse to linger in the stable though Veronica's note, now thrust with Sister Magdalen's Spiritual Notebook deep among the roots of the apple tree until a safer hiding-place could be devised, had asked her to be there after the general confession.

Going into the stable she was greeted by Lilith's reproachful snicker.

"I'll be with you directly, old girl." She switched on the solitary overhead bulb that provided the sole il-

lumination and jumped slightly as Veronica's slight form
rose from behind the feed-bag where she had been
crouched.

"I slipped away early," the girl said. "You didn't tell
anyone?"

"Not yet." Sister Joan decided that remaining cool
and calm in the face of the girl's obvious agitation was
the wisest course of action. "Sit down, child, and keep
your voice low though I doubt if anyone will hear us. I
have the mare to feed."

"I came early and left a bolster in my bed," Veronica said breathlessly, sitting on the bench against the
wall. "I want to get back before they finish confessions.
I was praying you would get out early."

"More by accident than design," Sister Joan told her,
fitting on Lilith's nosebag and deciding to delay the
grooming. "You had no right to send such a note, you
know, and I have no right to be here. I'm assuming that
you can't confide in anyone else?"

"I don't know whom to trust," Veronica said gulp-
ingly. "You're new here like me so you might not realise what's going on. I don't understand it myself."

"What exactly don't you understand?"

Sister Joan went over to the bench and sat down at
the other end of it.

"I wanted to be a nun for ages," Veronica said. "My
parents have never been keen on the idea but ever since
I left school I've wanted to enter the religious life. I
was quite ready for all the sacrifices and hardships."

"None of us is really ready you know," Sister Joan
interjected. "We only think we are."

"But there aren't any," Veronica said. "Not really,
Sister. Oh, one has to stay in the Novitiate and go everywhere with Sister Hilaria or Mother Emmanuel, but
I expected that. I expected to have to pray and meditate
a lot and be scolded for small faults. That's all part of

the training. But the other things—Sister, I don't know how different the Order of the Daughters of Compassion is from other Orders but I'd guess very different.''

"In what way?''

Veronica hesitated, then asked instead,

"Have you heard of a Sister Magdalen?''

"What about her?'' Sister Joan's voice had sharpened.

"She—oh dear!'' She broke off gaspingly as a shadow loomed in the open doorway.

"Johnny Russell, what are you doing here?'' Sister Joan expelled her breath in mingled relief and exasperation.

"I decided to have a look round,'' he said calmly. "The gates were wide open.''

"You had better come in and shut the door, and sit over there.'' Sister Joan nodded primly towards the feed-bag. "Sister Veronica was just going to tell me something about Brenda. Veronica, this is Johnny Russell. He's a friend of Sister Magdalen and he's anxious about her.''

"Do you know anything about her?'' Johnny lowered himself obediently to the feed-bag and stared at her intently.

"She left the convent back in February,'' Veronica said disappointedly. "Mother Emmanuel says she was very beautiful and the Order is fortunate to get an equally beautiful replacement in me though I'm smaller. I'm sorry, Sister Joan. I don't mean to sound conceited but that's exactly what she said—Mother Emmanuel, I mean.''

"Did she say anything about where Sister Magdalen went?'' Sister Joan asked.

The other shook her bonneted head.

"She and the Prioress just went on about how pretty

she was and how I must accept what God had planned for me as she did.''

"And what has He planned?" Sister Joan asked.

"I don't know, Sister, but it has something to do with the fifth Gospel," Veronica said.

"There are only four Gospels," Sister Joan said.

"That's what I thought," Veronica said earnestly, "but the Prioress told me there is a fifth one only just being translated."

"I thought Matthew, Mark, Luke and John were the Gospels," Johnny put in.

"The only ones accepted as authentic by the Church," Sister Joan nodded. "There is a Gospel of Thomas and a Gospel of Peter but neither has been accepted as authentic. They are among the Apochrypha.''

"This isn't any of them," Veronica said. "It's the Gospel of the Blessed Virgin she says."

"The Blessed Virgin never wrote a Gospel."

"Apparently She did," Veronica said, "and all the doctrines of the Church will have to be revised when the translation is finally published. At the moment it's a great secret to all but a few of the professed Sisters and to Sister Felicity. Even the other novices haven't been told."

"Told what?" Sister Joan pressed. "What have you been told, Veronica?"

"Only that I've been chosen," Veronica said. "Reverend Mother Ann said I was a favoured handmaid of the Lord and that at Solstice the Gabriel will come. I don't know what she was talking about, Sister, but it bothers me. It bothers me that we none of us had to have our hair cut off. I thought that novices always did."

"They do," Sister Joan muttered.

She herself was more bothered than she was willing to reveal to the other two.

"I don't see what all this has to do with Brenda," Johnny complained.

"The chosen handmaid of the Lord," Sister Joan repeated softly and shivered, scenting heresy.

"It isn't like I expected it to be," Veronica said, "but I've never been a novice before so perhaps what I expected wasn't correct either."

"Your instincts aren't misleading you," Sister Joan said soberly. "Something is very wrong, very wrong indeed here. Johnny, let me try briefly to explain. Catholics worship the Holy Trinity but they pay great honour to the Holy Virgin. Not worship but what is technically called hyperdulia. She is first among all the saints and angels but she was never a divine being, though some of the titles we give her were originally given to female goddesses. A lot of Catholic belief and ritual is adapted from the pagan faiths of the past. But it isn't the same belief and it's been transformed by the ethics of Christian belief. It's like—like an old house that's been pulled down and a better house built on the foundations. We all know the foundations are there but we aren't forever poking about in the cellars or taking people down there to live. Do you follow me?"

"So far." He nodded.

"Devotion to the Blessed Virgin cannot be allowed to supersede worship of God," Sister Joan continued. "In this convent there is a decided leaning to more primitive and extreme forms of Mariolatry. This idea of a fifth gospel written by the Holy Virgin Herself is—I never heard of such a thing. I don't know where Brenda's disappearance fits in with all this, I could perhaps fit it all together if I knew more about this so-called fifth Gospel."

She broke off, tapping her thumbnail against her teeth.

"Reverend Mother Ann didn't show it to me," Veronica said.

"I'm not very interested in the theology of it," Johnny said impatiently. "I want to find Brenda and if she hasn't turned up by lunchtime on Monday then I'm going to the police."

"Maybe she got frightened and ran away," Veronica said. "There is something a bit frightening about the Prioress. I can't explain what I mean exactly because she's always so pleasant but there's something at the back of her eyes—as if she knew something nobody else knew and it was making her laugh inside."

"Veronica, do you think you can slip back to the Novitiate and carry on as usual?" Sister Joan asked.

"I think so." Veronica sounded doubtful.

"Solstice isn't for three weeks yet," Sister Joan reminded her. "Whatever is going to happen will happen then."

"What is this Solstice?" Johnny enquired.

"There are four ancient feasts when the quarters of the year are divided by the changing of one astrological sign into another," Sister Joan said. "Two solstices and two equinoxes. In pagan times when society was largely agricultural they were important landmarks in the year. There's a local festival here on that day with a procession and dancing—all very rustic and innocent. What else has been planned by Reverend Mother Ann I don't know."

"I do know where the fifth Gospel is kept," Veronica said unexpectedly.

"Where?" Sister Joan looked at her sharply.

"In the base of the statue of Our Lady in the parlour," the girl said. "I went there for the private talk she wanted and I was a few minutes early. The door was ajar and she was putting some papers in the base. There's a kind of drawer there. I'm sure it was the Gospel because later on she told me that the translation was quite safe because it was at the feet of the Holy Virgin.''

"Thank you, Veronica." Sister Joan reached out to pat the girl's shoulder. "Now hurry back and get into bed and try not to worry too much. You did absolutely right to tell me." Veronica nodded, murmured a polite excuse-me to Johnny and flitted out into the darkness.

"Johnny." Sister Joan hesitated, then went on. "Can you do some research for me in Bodmin? Find out as much as you can about the Tarquin family. Grant Tarquin's father was the one who sold Cornwall House to the Order when the family went broke. Fine out everything you can about them, about him in particular. Make a proper report of it and meet me—"

"At the school?"

"Before Monday." She bit her lip, thinking. "Look, on Sunday afternoons we have free time, when we can write letters or read or go for a walk. At the back of the enclosure, outside the wall there's a kind of dip with hawthorn bushes all around. I'll meet you there, sometime between two and four. I can't be more accurate than that."

"Sunday then." He rose, looking down at her for a moment. When he spoke his voice sounded adult and sad. "You think Brenda's dead, don't you?" he said.

"I don't know, Johnny," she said honestly. "I'd like to believe that she really is on some Welsh commune because the alternative terrifies me, but I don't know."

"I'll see you on Sunday," Johnny said, and left the stable.

Sister Joan rose, her limbs heavy with reluctance. They would still be at general confession which gave her what might be the only opportunity to get hold of this so-called fifth Gospel. She would have to keep it for a couple of days and pray that Reverend Mother Ann didn't require it.

The door of the parlour was unlocked. She switched on the overhead light and crossed to the statue. Isis/Mary stared ahead, remote and perfect. To her relief the drawer in the base, invisible until one knelt on a level with it, slid out easily. The typescript within was obviously Mother Ann's own translation of the coded transliteration left by her father. She had no idea where the original might be, and not time to speculate. There was time only to slide shut the drawer, turn off the light, and scoot at a speed definitely frowned on in convents up the stairs and into her cell where she laid the typescript under her mattress before returning to the dining-room in time to hear Sister Dorothy accuse herself of finishing the page of an absorbing book after the Meditation bell had rung.

Slipping into her place, Sister Joan found herself praying fervently that no greater sin remained unconfessed among the other members of the Community.

FOURTEEN

✠ ✠ ✠

Saturday was general cleaning day in accordance with
the rules laid down by the Foundress. Every nun, professed or lay, scrubbed down her cell, took her linen to
the laundry room, made up her narrow bed with fresh
sheets and changed her underwear for the second time
in a week. Everything that could be polished was polished twice including shoes and those who needed a
hair-trim queued meekly outside one of the bathrooms
where Sister Margaret wielded a large pair of scissors.
Sister Felicity had driven into Bodmin to collect the
weekly groceries taking Sister Lucy with her on a visit
to the dentist. Sister Joan had hoped that the Prioress
would accompany them but Reverend Mother Ann was
everywhere in evidence throughout the long morning,
popping in and out of the cells to admonish and praise,
calling on Sister Martha who finished her own cleaning
first to help her cope with her linoleum.

"The one thing I could never endure was getting the
marks off linoleum, Sister. You have done yours so
beautifully!"

Sister Joan, vigorously rubbing her window, thought
nostalgically of Reverend Mother Agnes, an apron tied

round her gaunt figure, as she silently and painstakingly cleaned and polished without delegating a single task.

At least Reverend Mother Ann didn't carry out inspections as carefully as the other. The slim typescript in its transparent plastic cover lay snugly under the mattress.

In the afternoon there were the weekly diaries to be written up and given to the Prioress. Writing her own bald and censored account Sister Joan wondered what would happen if she were to log exactly what her movements had been during her first week at Cornwall House. Saturday afternoon was also Visitors' Day when family and friends might call. The novices were, of course, debarred from this privilege and must spend the day cleaning the Novitiate. She wondered if Veronica's anxieties had been relieved by the confidences she had made. And had Johnny found out anything that would explain Grant Tarquin's close and protective interest in the Community?

On Saturday afternoons letters were distributed. There were none for her as yet, but her letter to Reverend Mother Agnes would only just have arrived and in any case she was sure her former prioress would answer with care since Reverend Mother Ann would see the letter first.

After the diaries were written up and handed in the Sisters were required to complete any tasks left undone during the week which gave her the first chance she had had of slipping away to read the typescript. She decided that the place where she was least likely to be disturbed was in one of the storerooms on the same floor as the library, and arming herself with her sketch-pad into which she slipped the typescript she made her way into the chapel and thence up the narrow staircase to the storey above.

The library itself was deserted. She paced on down

the corridor and opened the end door. This was the room into which she had climbed in her desire to find out what was going on in the chapel. Pale sunlight streaked the floorboards and the packing-cases provided more than one niche where she could sit out of sight of anyone who might open the door or, passing below, glance up at the window.

Tucking her habit underneath her she settled herself comfortably and drew a deep breath to still the sudden trembling of her hands.

The typescript began with what was clearly part of a longer biographical work on Dr. Gillespie.

"My father's travels which were extensive in his youth centred upon the Near East during the last years of his life and were largely concentrated on the thesis he was planning concerning the survival of mother goddess cults after the advent of Christianity. I travelled with him during that period and was often entrusted with the task of transcribing certain manuscripts that fell into his hands.

"When the manuscript shortly to be considered was given to him, however, I was suffering from an attack of malaria which necessitated my returning to London to undergo an intensive course of treatment. When I returned to the dig he was engaged upon a new project and did not discuss with me any recent findings as he usually did.

"I was at that time seriously considering entering the religious life and my father's death some months later though a great grief did release me in a sense from my duty to him. His Will made me outright heir to his estate, a handsome dowry to bring into the Order. His private papers and unfinished research were not, however, released for my study for a further fifteen years.

"Accordingly not until five years ago was I given a mass of part translated and coded work, the fruit of the last months of his career. I had previously resolved to complete any unfinished work left by my father and this has occupied what time I have been able to spare from my religious duties in the past five years.

"The manuscript translated from the original Aramaic into his own private code by my father was, according to his own notes, given to him by a member of the Druse community, an elder living on the border between Lebanon and Northern Israel. The man informed my father that he felt the script ought to be given to an accredited scholar who would estimate its value. The manuscript which my father was constrained to smuggle back to Great Britain was, he states in his diary, 'the most explosive document that ever passed through my hands. If ever made public the consequences to the doctrines of Christianity might be incalculable.'

"For that reason he left the translation in his own private code and my own translation is based upon that code. For the moment I do not intend to make it public. I am of the opinion that to do so might distress those who are bound by the beliefs of conventional Christianity. I am also of the opinion that it was something more than mere chance that placed this document in my hands and thus in the hands of the Order. My own fervent belief is that the New Age will find its beginning within the confines of the Order of the Daughters of Compassion."

Sister Joan paused, read over again what she had just skimmed, and frowned. So far the provenance of the original manuscript seemed straightforward enough. There were, she knew, many ancient parchments in the Near and Middle East, many of them untranslated, containing a wealth of information about post and pre-Christian civilisations. The discovery of the Dead Sea Scrolls had unleashed a flood of antique writings of varying value, many of them still buried in obscure libraries or in private collections.

The translation began on the next page. Reading it slowly she was conscious within herself of an instinctive denial of the words that her eye scanned. It looked correct, but her beliefs and training rebelled against the implications.

"Hear, good people, the witness of Miriam wife of Joshua and mother of the Lord. This witness I give to Lucas, a follower of the Lord.

"When I was a child I danced and sang in the temple of the great mother and from that time was set apart to await the coming of the god. I alone among the maidens awaited the coming of the god in the person of the messenger, the Gabriel.

"On the night appointed when Virgin and Scorpion changed places in the heavens the older women came for me and we descended into the cave of beginnings where only the high initiates might go. Then came the Gabriel with his horn of plenty and to that mystery was I made privy that the Holy Child might be conceived and born and die for the sake of the world. More I cannot say for these are forbidden things.

"Then was I espoused to Joshua and my seat in the temple left vacant. This is the law.

"Once in two thousand years is the great rite enacted. Blessed and cursed is she who is chosen to bear the flame. Cursed and blessed is she who meets the Gabriel."

The rest of the page was blank. Sister Joan forced herself to reread it and went on to the final page.

"The foregoing Gospel was among my late father's coded papers and has been translated by me. The original manuscript is also in my possession and will remain until the time when it is ripe to be given to the general public. That may not be for many years since

in my experience the Church has always been slow to
accept new evidence or to incorporate it into revealed
doctrine. Indeed I incline more and more to the opinion
that this knowledge did not fall into my hands by chance
and that it was not through the workings of chance that
I was drawn to enter the Order of the Daughters of
Compassion.

"It is now my task to choose those who will accept
and translate into action that which is prophesied in the
foregoing Gospel. I must bear in mind that through
temperament and training most religious women are
conservative, distrusting innovation save when sanc-
tioned by a male-dominated ecclesiastical authority. I
must also remember that it is no virtue to shirk a responsibility even if the consequences be heavy. In every
organisation there is the inner court of those who know
the reality behind the symbols."

The final pages were notes made on what Sister Joan
surmised had been Reverend Mother Ann's choice for
her "inner court."

"i) Mother Emmanuel. B. 1932. Entered the Order
1952. Professed 1957. Novice Mistress 1968–73
when I had the honour of training under her. Prioress 1973–8 and 1978–9 when an attack of angina
forced her to resign. A woman of strong and res-
olute character, aware of the low status afforded to
women within the church hierarchy."

Also in love with her former novice, Sister Joan
supplied mentally, and quite willing to indulge any
of her fantasies if it kept her in close proximity
with her.

"ii) Sister Lucy. B. 1958. Professed 1983. A young
woman of delicate and charming attributes. In the
ancient temples such women would, I am convinced, have served the goddess. It is not, however

among the professed nuns that the handmaid will be found.''

Sly Sister Lucy with her false sweet smile and silent, gliding steps.

"iii) Sister Sophia. B. 1963. Professed 1987. Both Mother Emmanuel and I thought that she might be the chosen handmaid but her reaction to the suggestion was negative. She actually regarded it as a final test of faith. Certainly she cannot be relied upon completely though my requiring from her a vow of silence regarding the nature of the revelations made to her renders her harmless.''

It looked more than ever as if Sister Sophia's death had been the suicide that Sister Perpetua claimed it had been. Obviously she had been told something of the fifth Gospel, had rejected it, made her final profession and then discovered what? That the test she had regarded as academic was actually a course of action being carried out by her superiors? Had that been the motive for her suicide? The vow that prevented her from revealing the truth had made it impossible for her to prevent whatever was being planned. Had she told or hinted something to old Mother Frances in the days before her suicide that had led the old nun to write her letter to Reverend Mother Agnes?

Sister Joan recalled Sister Margaret's comment. "I told her that if the Archangel Gabriel came and blew his trumpet in her ear she likely wouldn't hear him, but she didn't laugh.'' The fourth name was that of Sister Felicity, born as the Prioress had noted in 1944, professed in 1972.

"A loyal and devoted servant of the Holy Virgin and despite her lack of higher education possessing a mind able to understand the importance of the female in the role of creation,'' Reverend Mother Ann had noted.

Sister Joan had reached the last page, obviously typed more recently than the others.

The two names on it leapt out at her.

"Sister Magdalen, B. 1968. Entered Novitiate 1987.

"Sister Veronica, B. 1970. Entered Novitiate 1988."

No record of Brenda's having left, no clue as to why the two names had been typed one below the other.

On one level it was frustrating and inconclusive; on another it was deeply disturbing. What was very clear was that Reverend Mother Ann was a woman in the grip of an obsession, and that she had drawn others into her own *idée fixe*.

"The problem with leading a celibate life," Reverend Mother Agnes had warned, "is that such a life is against nature. The natural, physical impulses must be channelled into other outlets, otherwise there is always the danger of hysteria or fanaticism. I am of the opinion that many who were named as saints would be regarded as mentally unstable if they were evaluated by psychologists today."

From time to time in the past there had been outbreaks of mass hysteria in certain convents, when nuns had declared themselves to be devil-possessed or had writhed in ecstasies that had nothing much to do with visionary experience and a great deal to do with sexual frustration. It was a danger against which every prioress worth her salt guarded zealously. It made sense of the apparently petty rules that discouraged personal friendships and made it obligatory in some Orders for the sisters to undergo psychiatric examination at stated intervals.

Sister Joan sat back on her heels, considering. The problem was that there was no Mother General of the Order of the Daughters of Compassion. Each prioress had, during her term of office, almost unlimited authority to interpret the rules as she chose. There was a higher court of appeal in the parish priest but the little she had seen of Father Malone convinced her that he was thoroughly charmed by the Prioress.

She slid the typewritten pages into their transparent cover and looked round for some place where they might be secreted. It would have been safer to return them to the drawer in the base of the statue as soon as the chance afforded but her own inclination was to hang on to what might well be the only evidence she had.

The huge packing-cases were nailed down but there was an infinitesimal space between their bottoms and the floor and the typescript could be slipped between the two. She slipped it there, mentally marked the particular packing-case and rose, dusting down her habit. Her next task must be to write a full and frank account of everything she had deduced to Reverend Mother Agnes and leave it to the other to take what action she deemed necessary. Having decided that she felt a rush of relief that made her feel positively lighthearted as she went along the corridor and down the stairs to kneel in the chapel.

"Entering a convent can also be a way of avoiding responsibility for your own actions," Jacob had argued. "If anything goes wrong you can rush to your Superior and dump it on her."

"Not at all. One has to work through one's problems as one does everywhere," she had argued.

Now, thinking back over the events of the last few days, she wondered if there had been justice in his strictures. In the outer world had anyone vanished as Brenda seemed to have vanished she would have called in the police by now. It was only the impossibility of connecting the convent with violence that stayed her hand.

Rising from her knees she made her way down the

corridor to the main hall. The front door stood open and Grant Tarquin's car was parked in the drive. Presumably he was visiting the Prioress since there was no sign of her as Sister Joan glanced in at the partly open door of the parlour and continued on into the infirmary wing.

This was obviously a good day for the three old ladies within. They were all out of their beds and drinking coffee by the fire. She stood for a moment looking at them, sensing the weight of their experience.

Sister Mary Concepta had entered the Order shortly after its founding at the age of thirty-eight, a late vocation unless, like Mother Frances and Sister Perpetua, she had transferred from another Order. Now, twisted by rheumatism, she was still alert and bright-eyed, her voice younger than the rest of her as she said,

"Which makes no sense at all. I am not in favour of giving in to popular pressure even in the matter of holidays."

"Good afternoon, Sisters." Sister Joan went in briskly. "Are you speaking of holidays?"

"Pagan nonsense," Sister Andrew said in her decided way. "Something called Solstice which has been revived locally by Mr. Grant Tarquin and encouraged by Reverend Mother Ann."

"In our view a mistake," Sister Gabrielle said. "Our own feast days are quite numerous enough to satisfy the most ardent desire for gaiety."

"It is always a mistake," pronounced Sister Andrew, "to allow a lay person even if they are a benefactor to dictate the course of action in a religious house."

"Do you know Mr. Tarquin well?" Sister Joan enquired. "He seems to take a close interest in the welfare of the Community."

"Some might call it interference," Sister Andrew said, with a sniff that indicated she was among their number. "We got along very well up to the last couple of years."

"Hasn't he always taken an interest?"

"His father was the one who sold this property to the Order and took a close interest in our welfare," Sister Gabrielle told her. "The son took no interest until the last year or so."

"Since when one notices," Sister Mary Concepta said sadly, "that many of the old disciplines have slackened quite remarkably."

"Perhaps the Prioress is moving with the times," Sister Joan suggested.

Three elderly faces were turned to hers.

"Moving with the times?" Sister Gabrielle echoed. "That is the last thing one expects from a prioress."

"The strength of Holy Mother Church lies in the fact that She does not move with the times," Sister Andrew said. "Rome does not bow to every whim of fashion. I know that's an out-of-date viewpoint. I am told that in some churches guitars are now twanged during the Mass. To attract the young back into the church they say. I don't agree with it."

"I always liked the sound of a guitar," Sister Mary Concepta said wistfully.

"A Spanish guitar can be melodious," Sister Andrew allowed, "but these modern instruments are all dangerous trailing wires and twanging sounds. Sister Joan probably has a different opinion, being so young."

"Not entirely," Sister Joan said, charmed to be regarded as a mere child. "I have attended an occasional folk Mass and they can be wonderfully inspiring, but I rather tend towards tradition myself."

"Mother Frances would have approved," Sister Gabrielle said. "She was very troubled in the last days of her life, very troubled."

"About the modern Mass?"

"Oh no, dear. Thank heavens we don't have that here yet," the other said. "No, she fretted about the novices. Having been a Mistress of Novices so often herself she naturally took an interest. She was not happy about Reverend Mother Ann's choice of Sister Hilaria—not that anyone can deny Sister Hilaria is a visionary. A most holy and dedicated nun."

"With her head up in the clouds three-quarters of the time," Sister Andrew pronounced.

"I imagine Mother Emmanuel is a great help," Sister Joan murmured.

"She would have made a more competent Mistress of Novices certainly," Sister Gabrielle said, "but her secretarial skills are so considerable that the Prioress was unwilling to lose them by confining her entirely to the Novitiate."

"We are gossiping in the most disgraceful manner," Sister Mary Concepta said, "but at our age the pleasures of gossip may be excused."

"But not at Sister Joan's age," Sister Andrew said primly. "Have you had a satisfying week with us, Sister? Do you find the schoolwork hard? It is often difficult to strike a balance between the secular and religious duties of our vocations."

The old lady had deftly blocked any further gossip. Sister Joan lingered to give them some account of her week at school with one or two anecdotes concerning the pupils which she calculated would amuse them.

At least she had elicited the pertinent fact that Grant Tarquin's close interest in the Community had only started a couple of years before at about the time when she guessed Reverend Mother Ann had been translating the fifth Gospel. She wondered if there was a connection between the two events.

"There you are, Sister!"

Sister Margaret's cheerful voice greeted her as she left the Infirmary.

"I went to see the old ladies," Sister Joan paused to say.

"They do so enjoy it when one of the younger sisters pops in." Sister Margaret beamed. "I sometimes think that the old go round in a circle back to childhood again."

It was scarcely an original thought but she looked as pleased as if it were.

"I am only sorry that I missed meeting Mother Frances," Sister Joan said. "And Sister Sophia too. She sounds like an interesting person."

"Too clever for me, I'm afraid," Sister Margaret said deprecatingly, "but very kind. She is a great loss to the Community. But there! God works in mysterious ways His wonders to perform. Oh, I almost forgot. There was a telephone call enquiring after you."

"After me?" Sister Joan stopped short as she turned to go.

"The Prioress—from your old convent I mean. Sister Felicity usually takes the calls but she has been delayed in town, so I took it."

"Nothing's wrong, I hope?"

"Oh no, but Reverend Mother Agnes said she would be glad to hear from you when you have leisure."

"But I—leisure has been fairly limited. I will write to her tomorrow."

"She sounded rather strict," Sister Margaret said. "Not that I would complain. With a strict prioress one knows where one is."

Sister Margaret smiled and went back into the kitchen.

If her letter had been posted the previous Monday it ought to have reached its destination within a few days.

Either Grant Tarquin had neglected to post it or he had held it back for reasons of his own.

Reminding herself that he was paying a visit to the Prioress she hurried into the main hall with some vague idea of waylaying him if she could do so discreetly, but she had delayed too long. Through the open door she glimpsed the tail end of his car disappearing down the drive.

FIFTEEN

✠ ✠ ✠

For almost the first time since she had entered the religious life five years before Sister Joan found the long services of the following morning hard to endure. Always even when she had been troubled by the doubts concerning her vocation that were common to novices the Sunday services had refreshed her spirit and reinforced her dedication, but on this morning it was impossible to enter fully into the beauty and power of the devotions. Rising, kneeling, sitting with her companions the same questions were running over and over in her mind like a tape that someone had forgotten to switch off. Where was the link that tied together Reverend Mother's translation of her father's notes, the unexplained death of Sister Sophia and the disappearance of Brenda/Magdalen?

The scenario building up in her imagination was one she didn't want to examine too closely because to do so would be to lay bare events that struck at the roots of her own personal creed.

"I never understood how any intelligent and rational person could ever believe in the Christian myth," Jacob had said scornfully.

He had rejected the Jewish "myth" too, but in the end it had prevented him from marrying her.

"If you have entered this Order in the hope of falling out of love," her Novice Mistress had said, "you have come to the wrong place, Sister. You will probably love more deeply and more passionately in a higher and broader sense."

But if everything in which she believed were found to be inaccurate then her sacrifice had been for nothing. She wondered suddenly if that was how Sister Sophia had felt when she had been initiated into the inner circle headed and inspired by the Prioress. And in that despair had she gone up to her cell and committed the final act of self hatred?

"The Mass is ended. Go in peace," Father Malone said, sketching a large and quivering cross upon the air.

Sister Joan rejoined automatically with the rest,

"Thanks be to God," and filed out for the midday meal which, being the Sabbath one, was more elaborate than the weekday meals with fish to vary the eggs and cheese that normally accompanied the vegetables and rice.

There had been occasions in the past when she had regretted the rule of silence maintained unless speech was absolutely necessary because it took an effort of will to save up some lighthearted remark or comment for recreation in the evening, but today the silence was welcome. She was certain she would have made only nonsensical replies had any remark been addressed to her.

The afternoon was free. What that meant in practice was that one spent a frantic hour catching up on the offices postponed during the week before. There was mending to be done, letters to write, one's stint of gardening to be fitted in, neglected prayers to be offered. Today she had only one object in view and slipped away the moment the final grace was said, pretending not to notice Sister David's hopeful smile. Her co-teacher obviously looked forward to a discussion on the sharing of their school duties.

Outside the sunshine of the day before had given place to a light stinging rain. The air was chilly and as she put on her cloak and left by the side door Sister Joan felt a sense of almost physical relief. Not many of the others were likely to go out which gave her an unusual privacy in which to skirt the grounds and circle round to the narrow dip of high bracken she had directed Johnny to meet her at.

He was already there, bundled in his anorak, looking blessedly young and tough. Seeing him was like opening a window on to the outside world.

"Have you found anything more?" he demanded without any greeting.

"You first." She trod cautiously down the wet slope, noting with appreciation that he had laid some plastic over a large stone for her to sit on.

"I went back to the Public Library and poked about there for the whole of yesterday afternoon," he said, perching on a similar stone. "The Tarquins used to be the bees' knees around here. They owned tin mines and fishing rights and farms and Lord knows what else, but old James Tarquin, the grandfather of the present Grant Tarquin, started drinking too deep and gambling too high and then his son, Grant Senior, got religion and started selling off what was left of the property to various Catholic organisations. There wasn't much left by the time he died. The present Grant Tarquin went into business and began improving the family fortunes again through his own efforts. He married and then his wife was killed."

"Yes, I know about that. A great tragedy."

"He left the district after it happened and went to the

States for several years. Then he moved back and built himself a very expensive house on the outskirts of the town. I got that from chatter in the local pub by the bye. The Tarquins are still regarded as squires in the neighbourhood. Grant Tarquin spends a lot of money and time on the convent.''

"And he never remarried,'' Sister Joan said.

"Never even come close, according to what they were saying in the pub,'' Johnny informed her.

He was looking at her expectantly.

"There is a fifth Gospel,'' she said. "At least there is a translation of what purports to be a very brief script either written or dictated by the Holy Virgin.''

"Gosh!'' Johnny said on a long, low whistle.

"Gosh indeed,'' Sister Joan agreed. "If such a manuscript were genuine then its worth would be beyond price. Unfortunately it's more likely to be a fake—not a modern fake. There were certain gnostic sects in the early years of Christianity who placed inordinate importance on the role played by the Blessed Virgin in the Redemption. I imagine similar manuscripts were circulating for years. Even the ancients faked things when they wanted to prove a point.''

"What does it have to do with Brenda?''

"There seems to be an inner circle of nuns,'' she explained, "taking their lead from the Prioress and establishing—well, I'm not sure exactly what's being established, except that it's almost certainly against canon law. Sister Sophia, the nun who died, was one of those who were in it but it seems she was unwilling. It's possible that it preyed upon her mind and she committed suicide, God rest her soul.''

"Was Brenda one of them?'' he asked tensely.

"I understand so. She was replaced by Veronica Stirling—the novice you saw the other night.''

"I've been thinking,'' Johnny said sombrely.

"Brenda never left the convent. Nobody took her to the station. You said her dress wasn't passed on. She has to be dead, Sister."

"She doesn't have to be anything of the sort."

"Then where is she?" he demanded.

"Johnny, I don't know." She shook her head in exasperation. "I don't know. For your sake I hope that nothing has happened, but I can't be sure. The truth is that I'm not sure of anything any longer."

"I've been thinking about it," he told her. "You know when I look back to last year I can see now that Brenda changed after she went away to college. When she came back the feelings between us had changed. I didn't want to admit it at the time but there wasn't the closeness between us any longer. When I came down here to try to get her to change her mind I was annoyed because she'd thrown me over, but I wasn't in love with her any more, not really. You wouldn't understand what I mean."

"Oh, I've an excellent imagination," Sister Joan said dryly.

"Which doesn't mean I want anything to have happened to her," he said quickly.

"You know convents aren't hotbeds of intrigue," she informed him. "Mostly they're very peaceful and respectable groups of women living the devotional life. All the sisters are free to come and go as they please—"

"Not if they'd found out something so damaging that they couldn't be allowed to get out and tell it."

"That's melodramatic," she said uncomfortably.

"Then where is she?" He had raised his voice slightly but at a warning glance from her lowered it again. "Sister Joan, I'm not interested in old manuscripts and what goes on inside convents. I only want to find out where Brenda is. Can you give me one good reason why I shouldn't go to the police?"

"I think you ought to ring Brenda's parents and tell them everything that's happened," she said at last. "Then it's up to them to decide what to do."

"I'll ring them this evening. They generally go out on Sundays. Anything else?"

"Can you telephone my old convent? Wait, I'll give you the number." She reached in her pocket for a pencil and a scrap of paper. "Tell the sister who answers that you have a message from Sister Joan for Reverend Mother Agnes."

"What shall I say?"

"Tell her that matters at Cornwall House require investigation. Tell her that I did write but the letter was held back. She'll know what to do."

She hoped as she spoke that she was right. Reverend Mother Agnes would doubtless contact the Bishop but these things took time and meanwhile Brenda was still missing.

"I'll do all that," Johnny said, rising.

"And I must go back to the convent." She shook off reluctance as she too rose.

"When shall I see you again?"

"After school tomorrow morning. Thank you for all your help. I appreciate it."

"I wish we could find out more. 'Bye, Sister."

Watching him go it struck her that there was a new gravity in his bearing as if events were conspiring to thrust him towards maturity.

The fine needles of rain obscured the landscape. She looked at the moor through a curtain of rain that lifted occasionally to blow little squalls of water in her face.

The prospect of returning indoors immediately was uninviting. She retraced her footsteps slowly, reentering the side gate near the tennis-court. The windows of the Novitiate were shuttered. The relaxation granted to the professed nuns on Sunday afternoons was not offered to those still in training. Sooner or later she would have to find a way of getting Sister Magdalen's Spiritual diary back into the Library cupboard. She doubted if there was much haste, however, since the pages that might have provided a clue had been ripped out and it was unlikely that anyone would want to read the rest. For the moment the book could remain tucked among the roots of the apple tree.

Her thoughts had kept pace with her feet. She was in the enclosure near to the little walled cemetery.

Without any conscious plan she passed through the archway and stood, looking at the simple headstones. Mother Frances's grave and that of Sister Sophia were marked still by plain wooden crosses. The rain had soaked through the twin mounds blackening the soil below. In some of the stricter Orders the nuns slept in their shrouds and drank from skulls to remind themselves that in life was death. Both customs had always struck her as somewhat exaggerated. Nevertheless there was something attractive about the certainty that one day in what she hoped was the far distant future she would lie here among her sisters.

The two neat rows were as tranquil as meditation, their grass borders neatly clipped, their headstones washed clean by the rain. Sister Josephine, Sister Bernadette, Mother Mary, Sister Bridgit, Sister—

Sister Joan stopped dead, her blue eyes resting on two of the graves, her attitude one of tense remembering.

The letter that old Mother Frances had sent to Reverend Mother Agnes. She couldn't have quoted it word for word but some of the sentences had stayed in her mind.

"I think often of the pleasant recreations we used to have under Reverend Mother Mary," and, "How I wish I had the penmanship of dear Sister Bridgit O'Reilly. You remember her, I trust?"

Two names drawn apparently at random from the old nun's long life and affixed to comments that had made no sense since Reverend Mother had been a killjoy and Sister Bridgit an illiterate.

It had to be a coincidence, she told herself, staring at the two graves. Mary and Bridgit were common enough names in religion. Or had Mother Frances known more than she dared even to hint? Had she on one late night in February when it was impossible to sleep risen and made her shaky way to some door or window for a breath of air and seen—?

There was a small shed at the corner of the cemetery. She had noticed it on the previous occasion and guessed it contained garden tools.

Her guess had been accurate. Her hands, seeming to move independent of her conscious will, seized a spade and returned to the level stretch of rain-blackened soil between the mounds where Mother Mary and Sister Bridgit lay.

The soil was thick, clinging to the iron of the spade. Digging as the rain fell faster she told herself she was being an hysterical fool. Jacob had warned her she would end up like this if she insisted on denying her natural instincts. In a moment someone would come running out to ask her if she had gone completely mad. Despite the chill perspiration was running into her eyes mingling with the rain.

Her spade struck against something. Bending she scraped away the clinging soil, saw the worm-eaten leg, the hem of a dress that had been pale blue but was now faded to grey, soaked by soil and rain. The stomach-heaving odour of putrefaction hit her and she turned aside, retching, her eyes smarting.

She had neither heart nor courage to uncover the body further. Instead, shivering with nervous haste, she tugged the spade out of the soil and began to fill in the gaps she had made, smoothing over the space as if it were black icing on some spectral wedding cake. There was still soil scattered over the path. As if she stood aside and watched herself in a home movie she walked to the shed, exchanged the spade for a brush, went back and brushed the surplus back over the ground. As long as she continued to watch herself in the home movie she could hold back the terror that bubbled up in her throat.

Putting the brush back into the shed, casting one brief critical glance over the tidied earth, she walked back to the main house outwardly as calm as if she had just spent a placid hour strolling in the rain.

She gained the side passage leading to the kitchen and infirmary before her legs began to fail.

"I never faint," she muttered through clenched teeth, refusing to admit there could be a first time for everything, as she reached the tiny dispensary where Sister Perpetua was grinding something in pestle and mortar.

"Have you something for dizziness, Sister?"

The home movie was flickering into darkness and her voice seemed to be coming from a long way off. She wasn't sure exactly how it happened, but suddenly she was seated on a chair with her head between her knees and a wet cloth on the back of her neck.

"Now swallow this, Sister." The infirmarian's voice was soothing. "It's sal volatile. I always find the old remedies are best. You are exceedingly pale. Have you been fasting?"

Sister Joan shook her head, relieved that the darkness around her seemed to be clearing.

"You've had a hard week of it," Sister Perpetua's voice ran on. "Backwards and forwards to the school and having to get accustomed to a new place. Too much to cope with all at once."

"I need to use the telephone," Sister Joan said.

"Why, that's against the rules, Sister." The other looked puzzled. "Lay sisters and the Prioress are the only ones permitted to use the telephone. You sit there and I'll pop into the kitchen and get you a nice cup of tea."

Since her legs still felt too weak to take her anywhere Sister Joan sensibly refrained from argument.

The tea, arriving a couple of minutes later, was scalding and sweet. Sipping it she tried to think calmly and rationally.

Brenda was dead, as Johnny had begun to suspect, buried between two nuns whose names old Mother Frances had chosen to mention in her cryptic letter.

The police would have to be informed. At the very least someone in the convent was guilty of concealing a death. The thought that something worse might lie on someone's conscience made her feel ill.

"I think you ought to go and lie down," Sister Perpetua said, breaking into her train of thought. "I shall make your excuses."

"Sister Perpetua, you nursed Mother Frances before her death, didn't you?" she asked.

"She didn't require much nursing," Sister Perpetua said. "She was just old, you know."

"But she could walk?"

"Walk? Oh, yes." Sister Perpetua looked slightly surprised. "Very slowly and with a stick, but on her good days she liked to go out for an hour in the enclosure."

"The cemetery?"

"I told her that it was morbid," Sister Perpetua said, "but she said as she was due to lie there soon it would do no harm to explore the place. Very dry sense of humour she had."

"And just before her death she was troubled?"

"Like me," Sister Perpetua said. "I told you when

you came that there was something evil about. People laugh at evil now. They say it doesn't exist, but that is the final triumph of evil, you see, to convince people that it doesn't exist. She said to me once, only a few days before she died, 'If I were younger I would take action, Sister, but I'm too old. I want to end my days in peace, not stirring my finger in a hornet's nest.' Funny thing to say, wasn't it?''

But easy to understand, Sister Joan thought. No old lady whose life has been cloistered would want her last days ruined by police and questions and the dismembering of the convent where she had spent so many years. In the end her courage had failed her and she had left only obscure clues in a letter to her former novice, to quiet her conscience.

"When conscience and desire war together give conscience the victory," Reverend Mother Agnes had said in one of her homilies, "but be wary. Desire can often masquerade as duty." If she telephoned the police immediately she would be doing what society insisted was the correct thing, but it was what she desired to do. It was a shifting of moral responsibility. What conscience told her to do was to confront Reverend Mother Ann, to find out some part of the truth for herself before she called in the authorities.

"I have to see the Prioress." She stood up, relieved to find her legs were no longer shaking.

"You said you wanted to telephone," Sister Perpetua said.

"Later."

Walking out of the tiny dispensary she straightened her shoulders, aware that her face bore what Jacob had always called her donkey expression.

The parlour door was ajar and as she entered the antechamber she heard the step of the Prioress on the polished floor within.

"Dominus tecum."

The light, pleasant voice in response to her tap on the wooden panel.

"Et cum spiritu tuo."

She entered, closing the door softly behind her, kneeling briefly.

"Sister Joan?"

There was no change in the amused smile as Reverend Mother Ann seated herself at her desk, but she knew. She had read Sister Joan's letter. Not only read it but was spreading it out on the flat polished surface.

"I assume you have come to tell me about this, Sister?" Her tone was mild. "Mr. Tarquin visited me this afternoon and brought it with him. He is aware of the rule that all mail must be checked by myself, not a task that any prioress particularly relishes, but one strictly adhered to in all our convents. He was disturbed by the evident secrecy with which you had written and intended to post it, and after musing for several days very properly brought it to me. I have read it and I am disappointed. Disappointed and shocked, Sister, that you could behave with such deceit and lack of loyalty."

"I found Sister Magdalen," Sister Joan said.

There was an infinitesimal pause. Then Reverend Mother Ann said,

"What are you talking about?"

"I found Brenda Williams, the novice who was Sister Magdalen."

"She returned?"

"You know she hasn't because she never left." In the face of the other's bland, sweet smile, Sister Joan felt her own temper beginning to crack. "She's buried in the convent cemetery, Reverend Mother, so it isn't likely she'll be coming back. And you know because you put her there."

"In the cemetery? Sister Felicity took her to the station."

"Sister Felicity didn't take anyone to the station. Brenda never left the convent."

"I think you must be quite mad, Sister." The Prioress was shaking her head. "You know one of the reasons that I have relaxed the rules slightly is that I have always felt too much austerity can have a damaging effect upon the mind."

"And I've seen the fifth Gospel," Sister Joan said. "I took it out of the drawer at the base of the statue. I read it."

"Then you will understand," the Prioress said. "I was not sure, not sure at all, but if you were led to the Gospel then you are clearly one of the chosen who will bear witness in due course to the Second Coming. You are one of us, Sister!"

SIXTEEN

✠ ✠ ✠

Sister Joan had known many emotions but this was the first time she knew the colour and shape of sheer terror. Yet nothing had changed. Reverend Mother Ann still smiled, dark eyes amused at some private jest. Outside the window the fine spring rain fell steadily.

"May I sit down?"

Without waiting for permission she did so, holding the terror at bay by some miracle of will.

"Perhaps I have been misjudging you, Sister," the Prioress said. "It is natural for you to be concerned since you are not fully acquainted with all the circumstances."

"No, Reverend Mother."

"You know that I have been collating and translating my late father's notes? While he lived I was his amanuensis, always with him, always dedicated to our joint efforts. He often said he could not have managed without me. There was never any question of my ever marrying and leaving him to pursue a life of my own. It was a willing sacrifice, Sister. While he lived I wanted no other companion. The books he published were dedicated to me. It was all the reward I ever wanted. When he died the entire world became a darker, more hopeless place. I resolved to leave it, to enter the religious life. In the religious life there is that same quality of dedication we had both given to the archaeological research."

Sister Joan folded her hands together, listening.

"Ten years ago his notes and private papers were released to me under the terms of his Will. A great mass of writings of which I had no knowledge. I had thought we shared almost everything, but he had been pursuing a line of thought that was kept secret from me. It's possible that he feared it might shock me since I have been devout since childhood. But he had left it for me to translate. It took me almost ten years since my personal time is so limited, and as I worked so the conviction grew in me that this was a sign, a divine mark of favour bestowed upon our Order."

"In what way?" Sister Joan asked cautiously.

"The Second Coming," the Prioress said. "The Holy child returning to earth, this time to fulfil His mission and lead us into a golden age. And He would be born again of a virgin. Oh, I saw that most plainly. It only remained to choose the maiden."

"One of the novices."

"A young and lovely girl, dedicated to the service of God, waiting for the Gabriel to come."

"You expected an archangel to arrive?" Sister Joan asked carefully.

"An angel is merely a divine force, Sister," the Prioress said. "That force may be channelled through a human personality. I waited for that personality to emerge, for the chosen maiden to be revealed. Of course I was most cautious about admitting others into my confidence. The religious life is not conducive to originality of thought."

She paused, still smiling.

Not evil, Sister Joan thought, but madness. That was

what Sister Perpetua had sensed, and who was to say where one left off and the other began?

"Sister Magdalen was the loveliest girl," Reverend Mother Ann said softly. "I knew that she was the one chosen, and my instincts were right, Sister. By November she had been visited by the Gabriel and carried the seed of holiness within her. That was a wonderful moment when I knew that we had, through her, been favoured by the Great Mother, Her Who was existing before time began."

Her eyes were glowing now, her voice as soft as if she spoke of a lover.

"Are you saying Sister Magdalen was pregnant?" Sister Joan asked in disbelief.

"She was privileged," Reverend Mother Ann said. "Those of us who knew of it were filled with joy—except for Sister Sophia. I regret to say that Sister Sophia regarded it as a calamity. She brooded upon it. It was only with the greatest difficulty that she was dissuaded from going to the Bishop."

Sister Joan felt a pang of sympathy for Sister Sophia as painful as if she had known her. She could imagine only too well the dreadful dilemma in which the other had found herself.

"It was suicide, wasn't it?" she said aloud. "Sister Sophia killed herself."

"When the balance of her mind was disturbed," the Prioress said. "Sister Felicity and I found her, you know, and we decided at once that the circumstances must be concealed for her own sake as well as ours. If she had come to me I would have explained that miracles take no account of conventional morality. Our Blessed Lady had scandal to endure as well."

But she had dropped hints to old Mother Frances, Sister Joan thought. She had said enough to rouse the old nun's suspicions, and then unable to reconcile her oath of obedience with her conscience she had taken her own, lonely solution.

"Perhaps we were wrong to tell the tale that we did," the Prioress was continuing, "but it seemed to us kinder to her memory. There are those who cannot bear the truth."

If it was the truth, Sister Joan thought. A nun was conditioned to obey, to accept the word of her Superiors, but a young nun, just professed, still raw from the training in the Novitiate, not knowing whom to trust or what to think when she saw her own deep beliefs twisted into something else—for such a one despair might well have come.

"Brenda—Sister Magdalen," she said.

"So happy, so accepting," Reverend Mother Ann said. "Knowing herself to be blessed, visited by the Gabriel, oh she accepted everything so sweetly. And then what happened was so sad."

"What did happen, Reverend Mother?"

"She miscarried," the other said. "Perhaps she had had moments of doubt and been punished for them. If so she never confided them to me. She died, you see. They say that these days it is most unusual for a girl to miscarry and die, but we could not stop the bleeding."

"And you didn't call a doctor? You didn't even call Sister Perpetua?"

"There was only myself and Sister Felicity," the Prioress said. "We called Mother Emmanuel, a tower of strength. Devoted to me and so competent. She and Sister Felicity took care of everything. You say she is laid in the cemetery? Yes, they would have done all correctly."

And been glimpsed by an old nun who couldn't sleep, who must have seen something from her window that led her later to make her slow way through the enclosure, to poke with her stick in freshly turned earth. And then she had written the letter that had so puzzled Reverend Mother Agnes.

"We gave out that she had returned home," the Prioress was saying. "Poor child, in the highest sense that is quite true. But sooner or later her relatives would come to enquire. And you seemed very interested in her, too interested for a newcomer. I judged it wiser to mention a telephone call. We had already removed those pages in her Spiritual Diary that spoke of the Gabriel. There would have been nothing to connect her with us after a year or two. A scandal here would inhibit the work, you see."

"And Veronica Stirling?"

"The new Madonna," Reverend Mother Ann said. "Such a lovely girl, though still largely ignorant of what will be expected of her. She has not yet been fully informed, but then Our Blessed Lady was little more than a child on the first occasion."

It would happen at Solstice, Sister Joan thought, when an ancient fertility rite would be re-enacted.

"Now that you know," the Prioress said, "it will be much easier. We could not trust all the sisters with the secret. Of course after the Holy Child is born then slowly, slowly the revelation will dawn upon the whole world. But we must tread cautiously for a long time yet. Father Malone is of the old school, you see. He worships the patriarchal God and does not pay due honour to the Goddess. My late father was inclined that way. He saw the worship of the Female as something primitive, something to be superseded."

Not terror but pity, for a brilliant girl growing up motherless in her father's shadow, permitted no life of her own, turning her resentment into adoration of his qualities, and unable to live in the real world when he was gone.

"You are under obedience to say nothing," the Prioress said. "Our little circle has many little privileges not given to the other sisters. We are the handmaids of the Goddess and so set apart."

"Yes, Reverend Mother."

Rise and kneel and recite the traditional blessing, taking care to keep one's face bland and sweet. Madness must be humoured.

Outside in the antechamber she drew a long shuddering breath and then walked steadily down the short passage into the empty kitchen. The lay sisters were engaged in other tasks; there was no sign of Sister Perpetua.

Closing the door, crossing herself, she lifted the receiver and called the police.

Reverend Mother Agnes did not look out of place in the parlour. The parlour looked out of place around Reverend Mother Agnes. That was Sister's Joan's first impression as she went in and knelt for the greeting.

"You may sit down," Reverend Mother Agnes said. "These last two or three days have been difficult for you."

Unbearable, with the police coming, the Prioress breaking down completely to babble of a girlhood wasted and a second Coming, the police photographers and the psychiatrist, and the sisters huddling in small groups to whisper.

"It was indeed fortunate that Mr. Russell telephoned me," the Prioress was saying now. "I am very sorry that his search ended unhappily, but he is young and resilient. I have more concern for Brenda's parents. This whole affair has been a severe test of their faith."

"A test for all of us," Sister Joan said.

"Yes, it has its attractions, doesn't it? A new madonna, a second Holy Child, quite a feather in our caps

if the whole thing had not originated in the brain of a
very sick woman."

"Was that all it was, Reverend Mother?"

"You are referring to the so-called fifth Gospel?"
The older woman smiled slightly. "The original manuscript was in the library, you know. Reverend Mother
Ann kept her father's unpublished works in one of the
filing-cabinets there. Everything has been handed over
to the Bishop. His Lordship will doubtless make enquiries into its provenance in a few years, or his successor might. My own feeling, which is purely
subjective, is that the document dates from no earlier
than the fourth century A.D. and probably belongs
originally to one of the gnostic sects profiting from the
general confusion of that period to try to advance the
cause of the Blessed Virgin ahead of that of Her Son."

"There is no chance it might be genuine?"

"There is always chance," Reverend Mother Agnes
said, "but Holy Mother Church moves very slowly. It
may be not until long after our time that any scholar is
given the original document to study. It is neither your
concern nor mine. We are concerned with the here and
now."

"Yes, Reverend Mother." Sister Joan sat up
straighter.

"I telephoned the Bishop as soon as I had spoken
with the Williamses. As we have no Mother General
our final temporal authority must be the Bishop. He
agreed that I must come down here personally to see
what can be done. Reverend Mother Ann has been taken
to the hospital. If she recovers from her present severe
breakdown then she will be removed to one of our con-
valescent homes where some use for her undeniable
dedication can possibly be found. She has a very fine
and intelligent mind, Sister. It would be sad to have it
go completely wasted."

She permitted herself a brief sigh for the woman who might under different circumstances have been a great prioress, and spoke again.

"Mother Emmanuel is to go to our mission in West Africa. She has a lot of maternal energy that can be put to better use than humouring the vagaries of an attractive Superior. Sisters Felicity and Lucy will also enter other convents of the Order. The police have decided no good would be served by bringing any prosecution and the Williamses agree."

"Sister Perpetua?"

"Was constrained into obedience and has suffered greatly in her conscience ever since. She is an excellent infirmarian and will remain here. You understand that the other sisters have only received a severely edited version of events? Fortunately the infection (for so I regard it) had affected very few. For that we must give thanks."

The police had been discreet, Sister Joan thought, and rather to her surprise Father Malone had proved more able than she had given him credit for, informing the Community that they were, with one or two exceptions, to remain in their cells, breaking up the small whispering groups with all the authority of his cloth.

"The novices?" she ventured.

"I have granted Veronica three months of absence," the Prioress said. "The poor child is confused, having entered full of romantic notions, and now she finds herself uncertain. I have advised her to pray and to reconsider her decision. Young Mr. Russell has kindly offered to escort her home. A very pleasant if rather pugnacious young man, capable of great devotion to the right girl."

Nothing could have been more innocent than her face and tone but Sister Joan's blue eyes opened wider.

"The death of Sister Sophia will remain in the records as an accident,'' the other went on. ''When the revealing of a truth serves no purpose then the truth need not be revealed. There will be an election for a new prioress tomorrow. It is none of my business but I hope that Sister Dorothy is elected. She has a lot of common sense under that rather unfortunate manner and it will benefit her to spend more time with the affairs of the Community than buried in the library. There is also a certain abrasiveness in her personality that will benefit the convent.''

Slightly startled, Sister Joan pondered a moment and then nodded. Under little Sister Dorothy there would be no nonsense like nail polish and goddesses and novices with long flowing hair.

''I shall be travelling back to the convent tomorrow immediately after the election of the new prioress,'' Reverend Mother Agnes said. ''Fortunately this nonsense only began a year or so ago after Reverend Mother Ann discovered the manuscript in her late father's papers. The harm has not run deep, save for poor Sister Sophia and Sister Magdalen.''

''One cannot blame them,'' Sister Joan said. ''They were both bound by obedience.''

''But not to the exclusion of common sense,'' the Prioress said briskly. ''Obedience must be allied with intelligence. However, Sister Joan, I doubt if unthinking obedience is one of your weaknesses. You would not have run headlong into heresy at the bidding of your Prioress.''

''I hope not, Reverend Mother,'' she said soberly.

''There remains only the matter of the Gabriel,'' the Prioress said.

''The Gabriel?''

''The man who fathered Sister Magdalen's child. You had not forgotten him, I trust?''

''What did Reverend Mother Ann say?''

"Oh, she named no names," the older nun said wryly. "She babbled a great deal of nonsense about the archangelic force entering a mortal frame and I have not questioned the others. I have no jurisdiction over that misguided man since no charges are to be brought. You may wish to do something about it yourself—or not, as you please."

Her long rather melancholy features were wiped clean of expression but her eyes under their heavy lids were bright and wise.

"Thank you, Reverend Mother Agnes."

Sister Joan rose, knelt, and left the room, her gaze thoughtful.

She had been given permission to act as she saw fit. It was a measure of her Superior's confidence in her.

The school had been closed for the week, notes despatched to the various parents. In the convent a quiet that was still somewhat tense and shocked prevailed. She went out to the stable and saddled up Lilith who greeted her with enthusiasm.

It was a pity that she had not been given the chance to thank Johnny Russell or to see Veronica again. By now they would be on their way north, though Reverend Mother Agnes could easily have delayed Veronica's departure and escorted the girl herself. That she had not argued that her perception had seen another kind of future for the erstwhile novice. Sister Joan had intended to ride into Bodmin and seek an interview but the car was outside the school as she approached and Grant Tarquin stepped forward to greet her.

"Good morning, Sister Joan. I was beginning to worry. There are rumours that some upset has occurred at the convent."

Darkly debonair, his eyes piercing her, his voice concerned. How could she have fancied he resembled Jacob?

"They found Brenda Williams," she said. "The novice who left."

"I heard someone had been taken ill," he said.

"The Prioress has been taken to a hospital, a mental hospital."

"I am very shocked to hear it."

"No you're not." Looking down at him from Lilith's broad back she spoke in a cold rage that effectively cancelled out all other emotion. "You knew she was unbalanced, didn't you? You used that for your own purposes, after she confided in you about the document her father had left. She needed a man to confide in because her whole life before she entered the convent was lived in the shadow of a man, and she couldn't go to the priest because she couldn't risk finding out that the document was spurious and her father not such a great scholar as she had always believed. She told you and you used that knowledge for your own ends. You became the Gabriel, to seduce a nun, a young novice with a head full of moonshine. Why?"

For a moment she feared he wasn't going to reply. Then he shrugged, his eyes amused.

"It pleased me to be the wolf in the sheep-fold," he said.

"Why? Why?" She stared down at him.

"You think that I enjoyed watching my father hand over the family property to the Church practically free of charge? Most of it could have been saved, you know, if the old man had had any sense, but not him, not him. He bought himself a place in heaven with his generosity to your Order and I was left to work my way up from scratch again."

The smile had vanished and his voice was bitter.

"That wasn't the only reason, was it?" Thoughts that had been spinning in her head began to coalesce, words to spill out. "There had to be some other reason why you decided to use the confidence Reverend Mother Ann had placed in you, to become the Gabriel. Was it because of your wife?''

''She was the only woman I ever loved,'' he said harshly. ''We had given up hope of having children when she became pregnant. Can you imagine what that meant to us? I'd lost my family home but my wife was going to have our child. Until some half-baked Sister of Mercy crossed the road against a red light and my wife swerved to avoid her. Swerved to avoid a woman who'd turned her back on a normal life as wife and mother. That nun's stupidity killed my wife and child. After that I devoted myself to making money, came back here, became the most generous benefactor the Church could boast. Waiting, you see, always waiting.''

No need to ask for what, Sister Joan thought. For a sick and twisted chance of revenge, offered him by an unbalanced woman and her little group of hero-worshippers.

''You were the Gabriel,'' she said.

''I was so damned convincing that I almost believed it myself,'' he said. ''They were wittering on about a second Holy Child and a new Madonna and all I knew was that there was one virgin less in a convent.''

''Did you know that Sister Magdalen was pregnant when she died?''

Her question had struck home. He stared at her.

''They told me she left,'' he said slowly. ''Now there are tales going around of a nun being found dead. Nobody mentioned—''

''It isn't something that's going to be broadcast,'' she told him. ''They didn't tell you then. After you had your sick pleasure she miscarried of your child. Maybe Reverend Mother Ann hesitated about telling you in case you decided not to carry on with what she wanted. That

novice you crept in to see died, Mr. Tarquin. She had
nothing to do with the death of your wife and your
unborn child. She was just a romantic girl, trapped by
her vow of obedience into going along with what the
Prioress wanted. And she miscarried and died. And
you have to go on living with that.''

"You think I won't find some way to forget?'' His
smile was defiant.

"Nobody," said Sister Joan out of the hardness within
her, "cares much what you do. The game's over and
nobody won."

For an instant he raised his hand and she gripped
Lilith's rein more tightly, fearing he intended to pull
her down, but his hand dropped again to his side and
he flung himself behind the wheel of his car and drove
off as if the devils of hell chattered in his ear. She
wished she could feel pity for him but there was nothing
within her but a sick and weary thankfulness that it was
over.

The following week the school would reopen after
the unexpected holiday and she and Sister David would
divide the teaching between them. The election of the
new prioress would be over, and—

Musing she trotted slowly back down the broad track,
concentrating upon the flowers that carpeted the moor,
laying aside the image of a vengeful man chased by his
private demons, a nun babbling of Second Comings, a
novice laid in earth.

"Have you taken Lilith for a ride?"

Sister Perpetua always stated the obvious. She stood
now at the gates, her reddish brows knitting together
furiously, blossom in her hands.

"For the chapel?" Sister Joan dismounted, looping
the reins over her arm.

"Sister Katherine is to share the duties of sacristan
with me for the time being. I always thought it one of

the nicest jobs in the convent," Sister Perpetua said. "I have a feeling that everything is going to be very different from now on, more like my old convent."

"Shall I come with you to the chapel, Sister? I've some praying to do on my own account," Sister Joan said.

For a man who wasn't really like Jacob at all, and an old nun who had seen more than she had had strength to tell, and a young couple making their way north. For them in particular.

"The rain's stopped," she said. "Summer's on the way. Isn't that grand?"

ABOUT THE AUTHOR

Veronica Black is the pseudonym of an author living in England.